STONE FACE

A STONE COLD THRILLER

J.D. WESTON

WESTON MEDIA

STONE FACE

CHAPTER ONE

"One click of that button, Herman," said Lucas, as he tugged at the small growth of hair he was cultivating on his chin. "That's all it takes."

Herman Hoffman held his head in his hands, squeezing his ears to stop Lucas' taunting voice. The green light from the computer screen was bright in the dark room and, on the screen, monochrome cars sat in lines of traffic while pedestrians fought a perpetual battle for pavement space without breaking momentum.

"I can't," said Herman. "You can't make me do this. It is not right. It is inhuman."

Lucas raised his hand to Herman's face, stroking his skin and caressing the outside of his ear.

"I think we both know that's not true, dear Herman," replied Lucas, and twisted Herman's face towards the closed door on the far side of the room. "How do you think the lovely Martina would feel about that? What do you think she will say when I tell her that her poor dear Herman has failed?"

"Stop it," said Herman, covering his face with his fingers, and peering through the gap at the door. "Just stop it all."

"She thinks you're a failure anyway, doesn't she, Herman? Why else would she do what she did? Why else would she fall into the arms of another man?"

"You don't know that. You have no proof."

A vein, blue and thick, stuck from Lucas' left temple, and his eye twitched twice, followed by the left side of his mouth as if in reply.

"I have all the proof I need, Herman," said Lucas. "The unexplained late nights, the missing money, and let's face it, when was the last time she kept you warm at night?"

"That's none of your business," said Herman.

"Well, I'm making it my business. If you can't be a man and stand up for yourself, perhaps I should. You're not going to let people walk all over you, are you?"

Herman stared at the door.

"No," said Herman, after a pause.

"So be a man, Herman," said Lucas with a grin. "Show them who's boss."

"Does it have to be this way? Surely there must be some other way."

"No," spat Lucas. "It must be this way and it must be now. Strike while the iron is hot, Herman. All you have to do is hit the button on that remote and your journey to becoming a man will begin. Albeit, a little late in life."

A tightness began to squeeze at Herman's chest. His eyes watered, stinging from lack of sleep.

"You do want to be a man, Herman?" said Lucas, running his hand through the tight curls of his dark hair, admiring his reflection in the window. "Do you want people to remember you as the man who stood up for himself? Or do you want people to remember you as the man who failed? The man who sobbed and wept and watched while his brother stood up for him?"

"But there's so many people down there," said Herman. "There's so many innocent people."

"Innocent?" said Lucas. His mocking tone accentuated the word.

"Innocent? Herman, you have so much to learn. Every one of them down there is guilty of something. Every one of them deserves punishment in one form or another. And it'll be you who delivers that punishment, Herman. It's nearly time. Are you ready?"

"No," said Herman. "I can't do it."

"So then, I must make a man of you myself," said Lucas, still admiring his own reflection. His voice quietened. "But you must decide who is first."

Dropping his head to his hands once more, Herman pulled at his hair, letting it run between his tight knuckles. Tears fell to the carpet and a low, monotone grumble grew from the back of his throat.

"Tell me," said Lucas. "I am losing my patience and the window of opportunity is closing."

"How can I decide?"

"Shall I decide for you?" said Lucas, allowing anger to slip into his tone. But then he caught it and softened his words. "Who should die first? Dear little Sam?"

"No," said Herman.

But Lucas continued his musings, regardless.

"He wouldn't even know it was coming. His neck would snap in my hands like a Christmas turkey, Herman."

"Stop it. How can I decide?"

"Or perhaps the marvellous Martina should go first?" said Lucas. Then he stopped and stared at his reflection again in wonder at his own imagination. "I might even have some fun with her before she goes. Now there's a thought."

Herman raised his head from his hands. The emotion was gone from his face, leaving nothing but anger and hatred in his eyes.

"You wouldn't," said Herman.

Lucas smiled at him.

"Oh, but I would, Herman. It's not hard to imagine what she looks like beneath those slutty dresses she wears when she goes to see her fancy man, her bit on the side."

Herman's voice lowered. He stood from the desk with his back to the door and stretched his arms out to defend his wife and child from the monster that plagued his mind.

"If you lay one hand on her, Lucas," he began.

"Oh yes," said Lucas, exaggerating his nonchalance.

"If you touch one hair on her body."

"There he is," said Lucas, stepping forward. "That's the Herman I wanted to see."

"Get away from me," said Herman. "Leave us alone."

"All you have to do is hit the button, Herman."

Herman brought the phone up into the dim light and stared down at the green call button, imagining the lives that would change if he pushed it.

"That's it," said Lucas, glancing at the screen and then his watch. "That's it, Herman. It is time."

Herman studied the phone as if seeing it for the first time.

Behind him, the door handle squeaked as Lucas pushed it down.

"I can't," said Herman, as Lucas pushed the door open to reveal Martina tied to the bed, her eyes wide and pleading. But the gag in her mouth prevented any sound other than a high-pitched muffle to escape. Sam was sitting on the floor. His hands were bound to the bed frame and a hood had been pulled over his face.

"So then, I'll decide," said Lucas, his voice dropping to a whisper. He stepped across the threadbare carpet to where Martina began to thrash against her restraints. He turned to face the window and let a serious look of hatred wipe away his delight.

"Stop it," said Herman, pleading with Lucas to stop the torment.

Lucas flicked at Martina's hair with his index finger then ran it down her face to her chest.

"No," said Herman. "Just stop it."

But Lucas' wandering hands were already exploring Martina's rigid body.

"Okay. Okay," said Herman.

Lucas looked up to the window, his hand pausing mid-action.

Martina stared at her husband. A look of dread filled her eyes.

"I'll do it," said Herman, holding the phone in the air.

Lucas smiled.

"So you've become a man, my dear Herman."

With his eyes locked onto his wife's in a look of apology, Herman pushed the button.

CHAPTER TWO

The driver's door of a silver saloon opened and a middle-aged man wearing a cheap suit eased himself out of the car. He straightened his tie, checked his reflection in the car window, then closed and locked the door. The indicators flashed on once simultaneously with the sound of the locks clunking into place.

"Are you ready for this?" said Melody, as she killed the engine of her little Mazda.

"How hard can it be?" replied Harvey.

"Just be nice to him," said Melody. "Don't scare this one off."

Opening the passenger door, Harvey climbed out, stretched his neck and nodded at the man, who made his way towards them with a smile that faded when he caught Harvey's eye. He diverted to Melody, his smile returning at half-mast.

"Miss Mills?" said the man, offering his hand to Melody, and then to Harvey who watched him walk around the car. Feeling the sharp end of Melody's stare, Harvey shook the man's hand. "I'm Jeremy. You found the place okay?" he asked. His thick eyebrows lifted as if two giant caterpillars on his face prepared to fight.

"It was easy enough," said Melody. "Thank you so much for

meeting us at short notice. We were keen to get the paperwork signed."

"It's no bother at all, really," he replied, offering a warm, practiced smile. "I really do think you'll enjoy living here. If you're looking for character and space, you can't really go wrong with Wimbledon. Are you familiar with the area at all?"

He stopped at the gate to hear Melody's response.

"Well-" said Melody.

"Yes," said Harvey, looking up at the windows of their new, rented house. "We know the area well enough. Shall we do the paperwork inside?"

Holding his hand out for the man to enter first, Harvey waited then followed the others into the house, ignoring Melody's warning stare.

"The place has been empty for a few weeks, but I'm sure it'll air out. It's fully furnished, as you know, so it's ready to move in," said Jeremy.

"Good," replied Melody, "because right now we're staying with friends. We'd like to start the new year in our new home."

"A fresh start?" asked Jeremy. "Nothing beats starting a new year in a new house with new habits. Out with the old and in with the new, as they say," he finished. But his humour failed to raise a smile on Harvey's face.

"Is there an inventory?" asked Melody.

"Yes, of course," said Jeremy, and laid his case on the kitchen work surface. He ruffled through some paperwork, muttering to himself.

"I'm going to take a look around," said Harvey.

"And leave me to do the boring stuff?" said Melody with a smile. "I'm joking. Go. Look around."

Harvey slipped out into the hallway and stepped into the living room. Large bay windows offered a wide field of view into the street outside. A large TV had been placed in the corner of the room in front of a leather sofa and two armchairs.

The high standard of finishing had been continued upstairs. The front bedroom, which was the largest of four, offered an en suite bathroom, a large king-sized bed and built-in wardrobes. Generic artwork of city life tastefully dotted the walls. The bedroom also featured a bay window with a window seat comprising of three purpose-made cushions to allow the occupant of the room a place to sit and watch the world go by.

Harvey didn't sit. Instead, he let his eyes roll across the Mercedes and BMWs that lined the street, noting how the South West suburb differed from the East London he'd known as a child, where the working class drove used cars. Only the wealthy could afford Jaguars and higher-end vehicles, such as his foster father who relished in the turning of heads as he cruised along the narrow streets.

The main bathroom was at the far end of the upstairs hallway. A built-in shower with a glass cubicle large enough for two or three people overlooked a roll top bathtub. The sunlight through the opaque glass fragmented across the gleaming white surface.

The back bedroom looked out onto the modest garden with a view of the side street where the line of high-end cars continued. Harvey noticed the long, unkempt grass and poor condition of the house behind, like a stain on an otherwise very affluent street. And in the distance, Wimbledon Common broke the pattern of houses and streets with its tall trees and seemingly endless green.

The front door closed and an excited Melody ran up the stairs calling Harvey's name.

"In here," he said, and continued to gaze out of the window.

Melody sidled up to him, sliding her arm around his waist.

"We should celebrate tonight," she said. "Our new home together."

But her eyes followed his gaze.

"Jeremy offered that house to us as well," said Melody.

"It's up for rent?" said Harvey, surprised at the condition. "It looks terrible."

"It's cheap in comparison to this place but would need a lot of work. It would suit someone. Just not us."

"I'm done decorating and renovating, Melody," said Harvey. "I need to settle in and relax."

"I'm sure we can manage that," she said, pulling him around to face her and closing the gap between their lips. "I think we should have an early night."

"I'll get the bags from the car," said Harvey.

"I'll pop a bottle of wine," replied Melody. "Then tomorrow, I have a full day of sightseeing planned."

"Sightseeing?" said Harvey. "Where?"

"London, Harvey. Do you know I've lived here all my life and haven't visited half the tourist places?"

"Do we have to see them all in one day?" said Harvey.

"No, but today is the first day of our new life together. I want it to start exactly how it will continue," said Melody, gazing out of the window at Wimbledon Common in the distance. "I want it to start with a bang."

CHAPTER THREE

Three photos were laid on the table in front of Detective Inspector Reilly. He turned them away from himself for the benefit of his suspect, Abdullah Nakheel, who sat opposite with his ankles cuffed to the chair legs and his wrists cuffed behind his back.

"You see this?" said Reilly, jabbing the photo with a shaky index finger. "Do you recognise her?"

Nakheel stared back at him through swollen eyes, but said nothing.

"Your wife, Nakheel," said Reilly. "Do you know where she is?"

But still, Nakheel remained silent.

"I can tell you, Nakheel, that she is not in the same location as this girl," said Reilly, resting his finger on the face in the second photo. "Your daughter, Fatima. Or indeed, your second daughter. In fact, we have gone to great lengths to ensure that neither your wife nor your two daughters are together. They are being kept in various government facilities across the city, and I can assure you that if you do not start to cooperate, they will suffer far more pain than you have done."

A tell-tale twitch of Nakheel's broken top lip betrayed his silence.

The movement, barely discernible, was caught by Reilly to use as a guide for further questions.

"Now, Nakheel, we have less than five minutes before the guards remove you. I'll schedule another interview in twenty-four hours. During that time, you will undergo more pain than I can imagine and great lengths will be taken to ensure your discomfort. But, rest assured, that whatever you endure, your family endures too."

Reilly checked his watch and pulled his sleeve down to allow Nakheel a little more time to think.

"Three minutes," said Reilly. Then he nodded at his colleague, DS Cole, who stood to one side and slid a single piece of paper onto the desk along with a black marker. "Write the name down. You don't even have to say it out loud, Nakheel."

He nodded at the guard to uncuff Nakheel's wrists then turned back to face the man he'd been hunting for more than six months. But even as the cuffs were unlocked and the man's arms were released, Reilly knew he wouldn't pick up the marker. Nakheel grimaced at the touch of the guard, squeezing his eyes closed to refrain from crying out with the pain throughout his broken body.

"Think of your family, Nakheel," said Reilly, softening his tone. "Have you any idea what will happen to them? Your daughters and your wife, alone, in a strange place." Reilly shook his head in disbelief. "How could you do that to them?"

The dried blood that bound Nakheel's lips released as he opened his mouth for the first time, defiant yet on the verge of a physical breakdown. He rested his bruised right arm on the desk. His left, which was turning a deep violet from the multiple fractures, hung loose. The pain was evident in Nakheel's expression, poorly masked by fatigue, at the thought of his two young daughters in a similar room with similar people in some other place.

"Your country," Nakheel began, his voice cracked, dry and no more than a whisper. "Your country is weak. You cannot hurt my family. You have too many rules."

The statement changed everything. Nakheel stared across the

desk at Reilly, confident in the protection the United Kingdom would offer.

"Cole," said Reilly.

"Sir?"

"Leave the room."

"Sir? I thought I'd-"

"Leave the room now, Cole," said Reilly, his tone sharp and impatient. "That's an order."

Brown eyes, set in deep ravines and cracked from the sun, studied Reilly's features, who shared the same weathered skin around his eyes, but which was a result of the beating cold wind and his own sins that kept him awake at night.

The door closed, leaving just Nakheel, Reilly and the guard who, at the slight nod of Reilly's head, stepped into action. He pulled a cord around Nakheel's neck and closed off his air supply.

Cuffs rattled against the chair and scrambled on the smooth concrete floor. Nakheel's one good arm shot up to defend himself, but the guard was strong and Nakheel was weakened by sleepless nights, regular beatings and malnourishment.

Reilly studied him, admiring his spirit and his fight to survive. So often, Reilly had seen men endure far more than he thought he ever could, which gave question to the strength of some men surpassing that of ordinary men. Or were they the ordinary ones? And men like Reilly, who would crumble at the horrific, tortuous procedures, were just weak?

Angry and gargled moans from Nakheel's throat sent spittle from his mouth as he fought for his life. Reilly checked that Cole had truly gone then pulled his hip flask from his pocket and unscrewed the lid, allowing Nakheel to watch him enjoy a drink while he died a slow death.

A flick of Reilly's eyes as he replaced the hip flask into his pocket was enough to tell the guard to ease off. From his pocket, Reilly produced one more photograph and lay it on the desk beside Nakheel's daughters.

The cord was removed from Nakheel's neck and the guard's firm hand dragged his body forward in the chair to look at the new photo.

"I'm sure you recognize him, Nakheel," said Reilly. Then he paused for the image to work its magic. Only Nakheel's rhythmic panting could be heard. A long bead of drool hung from his lip and touched the photograph.

Tears followed.

"Your son, Nakheel," said Reilly. "I didn't want to show you the photo, but I'm afraid you need to understand where you are and who you are dealing with."

With his good arm, Nakheel raised his hand and touched the face in the photo.

"He died in this very facility, Nakheel," said Reilly. "It's a shame we've only just found you. I would have let you watch."

Reilly stood from his chair and walked to the side of the dark room, away from the heat of the single bulb that hung above the desk. With a handkerchief, he wiped the thin layer of sweat from his brow, allowed himself another drink, and felt the warmth ease the shaking in his hand.

"Right now, Abdullah Nakheel, you are in a place that does not exist. You see the man behind you? He doesn't exist. And the men that come for you in the night to offer you their boots?" said Reilly, shaking his head. "They don't exist either. Your son is missing. Nobody knows where he is. His body will lie untended until the smell becomes too foul then it will be discarded like trash."

Allowing a pause to add weight to his words, Reilly watched as Nakheel's eyes traced him in the dark. His expression had changed.

"So please do not think for one second that you have the safety of the British legal system on your side, Nakheel, because right now, you're missing. And your family? They're also just missing. That's all."

He stepped from the shadows to reveal his serious expression to Nakheel, who followed him with new curiosity. Then, leaning close to the man who held the key to every Islamic sympathiser in London, Reilly whispered, "We don't exist."

Then he smiled at Nakheel.

A bang on the door broke the tension that Reilly had worked to build, and Cole took a single step inside.

"Sir," she said, her voice urgent and her sharp eyes flicking to the cord in the guard's hand and the red ring around Nakheel's neck. She handed Reilly a small piece of paper with three words written in block letters.

Reilly looked back at Nakheel, who let his head hang low.

"Take him away and make arrangements to relocate his family," said Reilly to the guard, and he saw the prisoner's brow raise in panic. Nakheel lifted his head in slow realisation of what was to come. "Maybe it's time we showed him how serious we are."

Reilly turned to follow Cole from the room, but just as the door was closing, a dry, weak and broken voice called out.

"Wait," said Nakheel.

CHAPTER FOUR

"Oh, you're good at this, dear brother," said Lucas, watching the computer screen as connections were made, encrypted and locked in place. "You're a technical genius."

"It's nothing," said Herman, his voice as quiet and humble as ever.

"Are you thinking about the bomb?" said Lucas.

Herman hung his head, shamed by the devastation he'd caused.

"It's just taking care of business, Herman," said Lucas. "That's the way you need to think of it. You're making sure everyone knows that you're not a coward."

Herman nodded and blinked away a tear.

"Have some confidence, Herman. Look at what you've done. How did you learn all this anyway?" said Lucas, fascinated by the way the screen had been divided into squares, each one showing a different CCTV camera.

"I..." began Herman. Then he paused and hung his head again. "I'd rather not say."

Lucas felt his jaw hang open then a smile curled the corners of his mouth like a snake with two tails. "You learned all this for your dirty little secrets?"

"Stop it," said Herman. "I don't want to go there."

"But, Herman, do you realize the power you have?" said Lucas, exciting himself with imaginings of what could be. "Can the signal be traced?"

"No. Well, yes. But it would take time," said Herman, reddening at the praise. "The signal is encrypted and diverted across Europe. The cameras are set to change at intervals, which means by the time they trace it here, the video feed would have changed and they'd have to start the trace again."

"You're a whiz," said Lucas. "That's the word. Like that kid at school. Do you remember him? The kid with the curly hair and glasses."

"I'm not a whiz," said Herman. "And besides, it didn't stop me being found out."

"But you learned, right? You learned how they found you before?"

"Of course," said Herman. "I have a trigger on a virtual firewall that will cut the feed if they manage to keep the signal alive, or if the feed doesn't change."

"See? You should be proud of what you can do, Herman. In another life, you could have gone places doing this stuff."

"In another life. Maybe," said Herman, and turned away from his brother's stare in the reflection of the computer screen. "I'm scared of getting caught. This is serious stuff, Lucas."

"With your computer skills and the things I learned during my little foray at Her Majesty's pleasure, there's no way we'll be caught. Besides, their eyes will be elsewhere. Every policeman in London will be out for him."

"But he'll be out for us," said Herman, his voice rising in both pitch and volume. He stood from the chair and faced the wall, turning his head sideways to find Lucas in the mirror, staring back at him with pure malice.

"I told you to watch your tongue, Herman. I told you to let me handle it. All I need is for you to do what I tell you. I don't need your cries. I don't need your worries. All I need is for you to listen to what I say and do exactly what I tell you. Word. For. Word."

Herman sighed and faced the wall.

"Do you understand, Herman?" said Lucas.

Herman nodded.

Lucas' frown relaxed, smoothing the pale skin on his forehead and softening his eyes.

"Come now, dear brother. Let's not argue. We've started it now and nothing can stop us."

But Herman remained silent.

"Herman, come," said Lucas. "We have things to do, people to see and places to go. It's going to be such fun. How will we find him?"

Breaking from his downtrodden slump, Herman stepped across to the computer table. He collected a tablet and placed it inside Lucas' rucksack.

"I can find him on here," said Herman. "I can remotely access the computer from the tablet. We can follow him without being seen."

"A whiz," said Lucas, winking in the mirror.

"Lucas?" said Herman, ignoring the compliment. "Can I ask you something? But don't be mad. I...I just need to know."

"Ask away, Herman," said Lucas. "I won't be mad, whatever you ask."

Herman pulled the rucksack onto his shoulders then pulled his hood up over his head. He checked the mirror to see how much of his face the hood covered then pulled it tighter.

"If he does see us, do you think he'll recognize us?" said Herman.

"My dear brother, if he does see us, it'll be too late for him."

"But what if he does sees us and he does recognise us? What will he do?"

"Would you like to do something before we leave?" said Lucas, averting the question.

Herman glanced at the computer desk then back at his own reflection. "You mean?"

"Yes, dear brother. Do it."

Taking the single pen that lived alone in the little, square, wooden pen holder on the desk, Herman opened the notepad. With a grubby index finger, he traced the list of names down until he found the one he was looking for.

"Say it out loud," said Lucas. "Say the name."

"Patrick Gervais," said Herman, pronouncing the name with as much clarity as he could muster.

"He'll never humiliate you again," said Lucas. "Say it."

"You'll never humiliate me again, Patrick Gervais."

"Good," said Lucas. "Now put a line through his name, and tell me who's next."

Herman let his finger slide across the notepad to the next name.

"Daniel Frost," he said. But the strength had gone from his voice. He glanced up at the bedroom door, picturing Martina inside and the times they had shared.

He pictured her with Daniel Frost and his emotions began to stir.

"Let's get on with this," said Lucas, sensing his brother's loss of strength. "Time's a ticking, dear brother, and our Mr Frost has a price to pay."

CHAPTER FIVE

"Stop," said Melody, and Harvey heard her stop in her tracks.

He turned to face her, glancing around for the cause of the outburst, and then gave her a questioning look.

"Come here," she said, smiling as she checked behind her, lining herself up with the infamous Trafalgar Square lions. She raised her phone in front of her face. "Come on, Harvey. Get in close."

"You want a photo?" said Harvey.

She thinned her lips at him, a sign there was no use in arguing.

He leaned into her and looked at the camera, but couldn't raise a smile. Beyond the phone that Melody held in the air, a security camera panned around and stopped when it reached where they stood.

The photo was taken, and Melody linked her arm through his and pulled him along.

"Come on," she said. "This is our day and there's so much I'd like to see. I can't believe I've lived here most of my adult life and have never been inside the National Gallery."

Standing beside her, Harvey eyed the people around them. Office workers and construction workers cut through the square heading in all directions. Tourists wrapped in scarves and gloves huddled close, both for the warmth and the safety against pick-pockets. A steady flow of double-decker buses moved through the heavy traffic. To one side of the square, a small lorry was parked and workers were beginning to build the barriers around the lions and other statues in preparation for New Year's Eve.

A crowd of people surged past. Harvey stepped out of the way and bumped into a woman who was rushing behind them. Melody apologised but the woman kept on walking, her head lowered to her phone.

He found another security camera in the opposite corner of the square. It panned when he moved and stopped when he stopped.

"Looks like we made it in time for rush hour," said Harvey, as three police cars with flashing blue lights cruised around the square, the lead car blazing its sirens. "Although they don't look like they're in a hurry."

"They're tightening security for New Year's Eve," said Melody. "I imagine the gas bomb yesterday shook them up a bit."

"It hasn't deterred the tourists," said Harvey, eying a group of teenage girls. One of them screamed as a pigeon flew past her head, to the amusement of her friends.

"How would you control them then?" asked Melody.

"Control the tourists?" said Harvey, gesturing at the hundreds of people around him.

"No. How would you control the terrorists who planted the gas bomb? How would you stop them? Millions of people are going to be standing here two nights from now. How would you keep them safe?"

Harvey smiled. "I'd go home and put my feet up," he replied. "I told you, it's dangerous outside."

"Oh, come on," said Melody, unimpressed by his response.

"I'm serious, Melody. I'm tired of all the drama. I just want to relax."

"Is the one and only Harvey Stone getting old?" said Melody, taunting him with her tone. She wrapped her scarf around her face and tucked the ends tight inside her jacket.

Harvey's smile faded.

"I'm just tired, Melody," said Harvey, and then grimaced as the group of girls nearby all began to scream and the pigeons flew around their heads.

"It'll quieten down," replied Melody, as the ever-present flock of pigeons took off.

The police sirens faded, leaving just the sound of the scurrying pigeons, which caught Harvey's attention. He tracked the nervous birds across the heads of the crowd, watched them circle once and then return to the feeding frenzy in the square, disinterested by the sirens.

"Shall we go inside the gallery?" said Melody. "It's getting busy here already."

But as she said it, a man knocked into Harvey in the bustling crowd. Harvey turned to watch him walk away. He was carrying a small rucksack and his face was hidden by a green hood that had been pulled tight against the cold.

"Leave it," said Melody, with her hand on his arm. "It was an accident."

But Harvey continued to watch him walk away through the crowd, sidestepping through people to the annoyance of a group of girls who called after him.

Harvey tracked his every move, waiting and watching.

"Harvey, come on," said Melody, tugging on his arm.

But Harvey remained where he was.

And then it happened.

The green hood turned. A pale eye found Harvey, offering a glimpse of one side of the man's face. Then he turned forward, put his hands in his pockets and worked through the endless stream of people.

Harvey made his move.

"Harvey?" said Melody, calling after him.

Turning and twisting through the traffic, Harvey side-stepped into spaces, cut between people, and moved others out of the way, his eyes focused on the green hood.

Melody was behind him, urging him to stop. But he had to know.

The crowd thinned at the edges, allowing Harvey to move fast. He ran into a space and scanned the area where he'd seen the hood last. Melody caught up with him and pulled on his arm.

"Harvey? What's got into you? I nearly lost you in the crowd."

Harvey didn't reply.

"Who is it?" said Melody, following Harvey's eyes as they passed over each and every person in sight.

A flash of green hood passed between a group of people. The face stared at Harvey then turned out of sight when he caught Harvey's eye.

"Him," said Harvey, and began to run.

"Harvey?" called Melody.

The hood slipped out of sight onto the Strand so Harvey gave everything he had, pumping his arms and finding a route through a group of tourists. He burst around the corner but found no sign of the man. Jumping onto the top of a small set of steps by a doorway, he scanned across the tops of heads, searching the pavement and the road. Then, on the far side of the square, beside Charing Cross station, the hood turned back to look at him.

Car horns blared as Harvey darted across the road. A woman stepped back in surprise when Harvey vaulted a barrier and ran across the road into Villiers Street, a narrow side road that led down to the Thames embankment. The hood, always one step ahead, ducked into a side street and began to run.

With his target in reach, Harvey gave chase once again. Running down the centre of the road, he followed the hood into the side street and through the gates of a small park.

He stopped.

A homeless man lay on his bed of plastic bags and flattened cardboard boxes out of the way of the flow of foot traffic, seeking shelter from the wind between some bushes. He watched Harvey with blatant curiosity through the steam from a polystyrene cup. His eyes flicked to the right and back to Harvey just as Melody came to a stop beside him.

"What on earth is going on?" said Melody. "Who did you see?"

But Harvey didn't reply. His eyes were locked onto a man at the far end of the small park, who nodded once at Harvey, turned and climbed into a taxi.

"Who was that?" said Melody.

Memories of a thousand faces took pride of place in Harvey's mind. Each one, he discarded and discounted. Too old. The wrong hair. The wrong gender. The wrong age. Too big. Too small.

"Harvey, talk to me," said Melody. Her tone dropped to a warning.

But before Harvey could answer, before he could issue the words he knew she was dreading, he felt a vibration from his jacket pocket.

Harvey stopped.

He put his hand into his pocket. His fingers grasped a mobile phone, its tiny screen alight with a sickly, bright green and the words CALL ME in bold, black letters.

Harvey glanced at Melody, who had begun to look worried. His thumb hovered above the green button.

"Harvey?" said Melody. "What is going on?"

He didn't reply. He hit the call button.

The taxi turned a corner at the end of the road, leaving Harvey with a glimpse of a pale face with a cruel smile.

A silence hung in the air like time had stopped.

"Harvey?" said Melody, growing agitated.

He scanned the park, listening to the phone as the connection was made and a dial tone began. The homeless man stared back at him. Tourists crowded around a map of London. Commuters walked fast with their hands tucked into their warm pockets.

A rucksack at the foot of a statue.

An image of the green hood climbing into the taxi played back in Harvey's mind. The man wasn't wearing a rucksack.

Harvey removed the phone from his ear, staring at it as the pieces came together like some sick puzzle.

"Harvey," said Melody, "what's happening?"

"Run."

CHAPTER SIX

An armed, uniformed officer raised the red and white tape that closed off the crime scene. Detective Inspector Reilly removed his cigarette, flashed his ID card, ducked below the tape, and then stood on the other side, not waiting for Cole, who was busy on her phone. The sound of her heels assured him she had followed and her sweet-smelling perfume arrived moments before her.

"We're looking for Connor," said Cole to another uniform, who was guarding the entrance to Belvedere Road and waving a Hazard Area Response Team through in their van.

The shrill sirens blared once to scatter a group of slow moving tourists trying to reach the London Eye. The young policeman responded with a gesture behind him, where Reilly saw the man he was looking for. At the end of the street, beside the entrance to Jubilee Gardens, a man in a long, beige overcoat braced against the wind and held his phone to his ear, pacing across the street. He finished the call, agitated as Reilly approached.

"I don't want to hear it, Reilly," said Connor, raising his hand, palm out.

"Not my fault, Connor," said Reilly, raising both hands in defence.

"Where were you twenty-four hours ago when the bodies were being removed?"

"Questioning a suspected terrorist," said Reilly, leaving Connor no room for a comeback.

"I've seen too much today for you to come wandering in and taking over, Reilly."

"What's the damage?" asked Reilly, ignoring Connor's comment. "I haven't seen the CCTV footage yet. But I understand it was an explosive gas canister?"

Connor nodded. "Poisonous gas," he said in confirmation.

"Well then, it's terrorism and it's my problem. I don't make the rules, Connor," replied Reilly.

He eyed the scene in the park. The uniforms had done a good job of sealing the area off, and the only movement was men and women in white hazmat suits with full face protection.

"How bad is it?" asked Cole.

But the look on Connor's face said it all.

"You'll need to suit up," said Connor. "HART have cleared the area for more explosives, but we're expecting the area to be reopened shortly."

"How many?" said Reilly, dropping his cigarette to the ground and crushing it with his shoe.

Connor eyed the cigarette with a subconscious look of disapproval, and answered in a similar tone. "Dead?" asked Connor. "Twenty-three with eleven more in the hospital."

"Has the detonator been located?" asked Reilly.

"A rucksack was found. It's being examined."

"What about suspects?" asked Reilly.

Connor's brow furrowed. He stared at Reilly as if searching for the right words.

"Have you got any idea what we've just seen?" said Connor. "Have you got any idea what twenty-three dead bodies looks like?

Have you got any idea at all how hard it is to control your own anger when you're staring into the eyes of a poisonous gas bomb victim? Fighting for every breath. Knowing it may be their last."

"I'm sure it's been a very trying morning, Connor," said Reilly, nodding and trying to convey as much genuine sympathy as he could.

Continuing with his stare as if in total disbelief, Connor remained rooted to the spot, his hands clenched and his nostrils flared.

"Trying? You heartless bastard, Reilly," said Connor.

Reilly prepared himself. He turned side-on to Connor and positioned his rear foot for stability. The signs were all there. Emotions were high. As Connor's shoulder moved back, his lower lip disappeared beneath his front teeth in a grimace.

"That's enough," said Cole, her voice breaking the tension just enough for Connor to relax his arm. She nodded at the small park ahead of them. "Sir, the hazmats are being removed."

Leaving Connor with one final stare to make sure the punch wasn't swung, Reilly turned to the park. Two people were walking out, removing their protective head gear and breathing apparatuses. They stepped into a large tent that Reilly deduced to be some kind of hose-down due to the water that ran from it across the street.

A sickly feeling gripped Reilly's stomach. Standing outside the crime scene was bad enough and having the jurisdiction argument with Connor was tedious to say the least. But entering the scene and focusing on the source, focusing on the facts and making a plan took mental strength.

He puffed his cheeks and exhaled loud enough for Cole to hear.

"Shall we?" Cole asked. It was a suggestion to move Reilly away from Connor with the subtle tact that she so often displayed.

Nodding at Connor, the two exchanged a look of understanding. There was no apology. The scene was stressful. The tension was high. And beyond their own personal disputes, people had lost their lives, while some still fought for them. They'd pick up the argument another day.

They approached the entrance to the park and flashed their ID cards at a man who was placing a used hazmat suit in a plastic container.

"You must be Reilly," said the man.

Reilly nodded.

"Jarvis," said the man, offering his hand, which Reilly shook. "The boss said you'd be coming."

"This is DS Cole," said Reilly, presenting Cole to his right. "You're HART?"

Jarvis nodded and cleared his throat.

"Are we clear to go in?"

"There's not a lot to see," said Jarvis. The lines of his face were deep as if they'd been carved into his skin. "No explosion damage and no sign of a device. It's like they all just dropped to the ground."

"Cole, get the CCTV sent across to HQ," said Reilly.

"The scene is clear. Whatever it was, there's no sign of it now."

"No residue on the bodies?" asked Reilly.

"The post-mortems will tell us," said Jarvis. "But it'll be a few hours before we get any results."

"No device and no explosion," said Reilly, verbalising his thoughts. "What are the symptoms?"

"Suffocation."

Reilly raised an eyebrow in question.

"They choked to death, sir. One minute they were all enjoying their lunch or walking through the park. The next, they were fighting for their lives."

"The survivors?" asked Reilly. "They must have been far enough away from the source for the air to dilute the gas. What's the range of the gas?"

"Thirty feet." said Jarvis. "The dead were mostly found beside the memorial. The survivors were thirty feet or more away." Reilly opened his mouth to raise a question, but Jarvis, an experienced investigator, continued. "The memorial is clean," he said. "As is the children's play park, flowers and grass around it."

An image of what the scene of the play park may have looked like came to Reilly's mind, substantiating Connor's words and demeanour.

"CCTV is being sent across, sir," said Cole, pocketing her phone.

"Good," said Reilly. "Have Connor and his men keep this place locked down. I want a list of the victims and I want a name to every face that walked through this place in the last forty-eight hours."

"I'm on it, sir," said Cole, walking away and retrieving her phone again. It began to ring as soon as she lifted it from her pocket.

"You're an experienced man," said Reilly, turning his attention back to Jarvis. "In your professional opinion, would you say this was a planned terrorist attack?"

Jarvis shook his head, biting his bottom lip.

"Without seeing the device, sir, I wouldn't like to say," said Jarvis, taking on a grave expression. "But I do know this. In two days' time, two million people are going to descend on London for New Year's Eve, and if we don't find the culprit, we could have something far worse on our hands."

It was as if the wind had dropped to allow Jarvis to speak. It began again as soon as he'd stopped, while the two men stood eye to eye digesting the potential risk the comment alluded to.

The tension was broken by Cole, who stepped between them. "Sir?"

"Yes?" said Reilly, breaking his stare from Jarvis.

Cole's phone hand dropped to her side, along with the expression on her face.

"There's been another attack, sir."

CHAPTER SEVEN

"Honey, I'm home," said Lucas, as he closed the door to the apartment behind him and pulled his hood off his head.

His tone hinted at humour, but his hate-filled eyes maintained their cruel slant. He collected an apple from a bowl on top of a cabinet and clicked open his knife. The bedroom door creaked open at his touch to reveal the boy still sitting on the floor, hooded and bound, and his mother, gagged, bound and staring back at him with bright red eyes. Her mass of hair clung to her face, damp with sweat and tears.

"Hey," said Lucas, leaning on the door frame. "What have you been up to?"

The blade of his knife cut perfect circles of apple, two inches in diameter. He took three steps to the boy, still holding Martina's threatening gaze, and licked his knife clean. Her eyes widened as he approached her son, and with renewed vigour, she fought against her bindings. Then she stopped, breathless and red-faced.

Stooping to place the slice of apple into the boy's hand, Lucas lifted the hood so he could eat, then cut one more slice and placed it in his palm. The boy's eyes were swollen with tears, his nose crusty with dried snot and his mouth a mess of dribble. He looked up at Lucas. The whites of his eyes criss-crossed with tiny red arteries.

"It won't be long now," said Lucas. "Your daddy just needs to clear a few things off his list. Okay?"

The boy nodded, locking eyes with Lucas with the innocence of a child.

"What about you?" said Lucas, standing, stepping away from the boy and facing Martina. "Hungry?"

Staring back at him, unsure of what her response should be, Martina remained silent. Her nostrils flared once and her eyes blinked away the tears that began to swell.

Lucas placed the apple on the bedside table, beside a novel, which was opened and laid face down to hold the page, and a small digital alarm clock. It was the type that had a large button on the top for the owner to hit and silence the alarm and large green numbers on the display that cast an eerie, green glow across the surface of the table.

She stared at the knife then back at Lucas, watching him unzip his jacket. He slid it off and laid it over the arm of a small wicker chair in the corner of the room. Then he sat on the edge of the bed and turned to face Martina with his back to the door.

"I'm going to release your gag from your mouth," said Lucas. "If you scream, it'll be your last. Do you understand?"

She nodded then grimaced at his touch as his finger slid the length of her cheek and pulled the twisted bandanna out of her mouth. He held it for a moment to make sure she kept her end of the bargain then dropped it to her neck and reached for the apple.

"Hungry?" he asked.

"Can I feed myself?" she asked. "At least offer me that dignity."

"Dignity?" said Lucas, as he cut a broad, round slice of apple. "How much dignity did you give Herman?"

"Lucas, you can't-"

"Do you want the apple or not, Martina? I haven't come to discuss the weakness of my brother and your extra-marital affairs."

"Where's Herman? I want to talk to Herman."

"Oh, no. Herman isn't allowed in here. You know the rules. He's weak. You'll convince him to set you free with your fork tongue," said Lucas.

"So why are you here?"

"To keep you alive long enough to see you suffer," said Lucas, his tone flat and direct. He popped the slice of apple into his mouth and bit into it, chewing with his mouth open. "Oh, and to give you the good news."

"Good news?"

"Your man," said Lucas. "What was his name?"

"Herman," said Martina.

"No, not him. The toy-boy. What was his name?"

Martina shook her head in disbelief.

"Daniel, wasn't it?" said Lucas, cutting himself another slice.

"What about him?" said Martina, her words staccato, as if she sensed the sentence Lucas was preparing to say.

"We killed him," said Lucas, and winked at Martina, whose face seemed to drop as if every muscle had been replaced, leaving her jaw hanging. "Well, I say we, but honestly, it was all Herman. He really is getting some strength. You should be proud of him."

"You bastard," said Martina, her voice a deep breath of hate. She tried to continue an onslaught of abuse, but emotion grew the better of her, and her voice whined to a high pitch then faded into tears. Prevented from rolling onto her side by the bindings on her wrists, she turned onto her shoulder and let her thick hair cover her face.

"I thought you might say something like that," said Lucas, pulling her hair away.

"Leave me alone," she snapped, and jumped into life. But her restraints stopped her like a guard dog's chain.

"Let's just pop this back in then," said Lucas, and pulled at the gag. Her emotions elicited some resistance. But Lucas pulled back a handful of hair and held her head still to replace the bandanna. "There you go," he said, and tapped her on the cheek.

He stood from the bed, collected his jacket and dropped the apple into the boy's hands without saying anything. Then he pulled the door closed behind him.

"How is she, do you think?" said Herman.

"Never mind how she is," said Lucas, taking a seat at the desk. "I need you to focus. Do you feel the strength growing?"

"I don't know," said Herman. He glanced at the bedroom door and then back to the computer screen.

"I'm so proud of you, Herman. Just look at what you've achieved," said Lucas.

"Look at all those people," said Herman.

He reached up to touch the computer screen. His fingers traced the outline of a woman who had fallen to her knees with one hand clutching her throat and the other hanging onto her baby's pushchair, her weak grasp slipping further until she slumped to the ground. On the ground in full view of the CCTV camera, a dozen or more people were fighting for their lives, including two paramedics in green uniforms.

"Roll the camera back," said Lucas, checking his watch. "Twenty-five minutes."

The footage rolled back, showing the woman with the pushchair standing in reverse. Tourists who were sitting beside the statue in the park popped up from the grass and sat talking.

A homeless man lying beneath a bush raised his head and rested it on his hand.

And Harvey Stone ran into the park backwards then stared at the mobile phone in his hand.

"There he is," said Lucas. "When you take him down, Herman, that's when you'll become a real man."

CHAPTER EIGHT

The doors of the train carriage seemed to linger for longer than Harvey remembered.

The noise of the crowds that followed grew, and as the first feet of the panicked stampede entered the tunnel, the doors closed with a hiss and the train jolted into action. Peering through the door as people banged on the glass of the moving train, Melody watched in dismay as the scared crowds grew larger, desperation etched on their faces at the realisation that yet another London bomb had exploded.

Then darkness, as the station fell away to the perpetual black of the tunnel.

The seats of the westbound train were empty save for a dozen people of various origins who all appeared to be traveling alone. The crowd outside was soon forgotten. Books were opened and legs were outstretched as the commuters enjoyed the less packed part of their daily journey. Newspapers covered faces and the noise through headphones was drowned out by the rumbling of the old train through the tunnel.

Only one man hadn't returned his attention to his paper. He

watched Harvey with inquisitive eyes that lay in the shadow of his long flock of thin, grey hair.

"What just happened, Harvey?" said Melody, moving close to be heard above the noise of the train. She gave a cautious look over her shoulder to make sure they couldn't be heard then waited for Harvey to respond.

But Harvey didn't reply.

"Harvey, this is too weird," she said. "How did you know to run?"

"Instinct," said Harvey. "It didn't feel right. He lured me there."

"Who was he? Was it him that gave you the phone?"

"He didn't give me the phone, Melody. He planted it when he bumped into me."

"So who is he then?" asked Melody.

"I'm trying to think," replied Harvey.

"Well, think harder," hissed Melody, leaning in closer. "It's him, isn't it?"

"Who?"

"The bomb guy from yesterday. They must be connected."

"Must be?" said Harvey.

"So there's two gas bombers now, is there? The odds are too small, Harvey."

"There could be three," said Harvey. "Or four or five. How do I know who's responsible?"

"Did you get a look at him?" asked Melody.

Harvey sighed and dropped to the seat nearest the door, gesturing for Melody to follow.

"Green hood, short jacket, jeans and black trainers," said Harvey.

"How about his face?"

"Just a glimpse. Not enough to place him."

"But enough to recognise him if you saw him again?"

Harvey shook his head. "I don't know."

Melody let out an audible sigh and sat back in the seat. "All those people in the park. Do you think-"

"I don't know what to think, Melody. Where exactly was yesterday's bomb?"

"Jubilee Gardens," replied Melody, as the train slowed for the next stop.

"The Southbank?"

"Right beside the London Eye," said Melody.

"Why would he attack there if it was me he wanted? I was at home with you."

"Whoever it was, they clearly tried to kill you, Harvey. You need to think hard who it could be," said Melody. "And how would he know you'd be in Trafalgar Square?"

"The cameras were following us. Well, me."

"What cameras?" asked Melody.

"In the square," said Harvey, trying to piece it together. "The security cameras."

"Why would the cameras follow you?" said Melody. "You don't exist. Remember?"

"I don't know. None of this makes sense," said Harvey, as the train rocked to a stop and the doors opened with a hiss.

"What's going on? We're not at a station," said Melody, looking from side to side out of the windows and into the dark tunnel.

"It's the security protocol," said Harvey. "They're shutting down the underground. We're being evacuated."

The other passengers closed their books and newspapers. Stretched legs prepared to stand and headphones were pulled from heads as each commuter carried a look of confusion.

And still the man with the long, grey hair stared at Harvey.

"We need to go now," said Harvey, keeping his voice low in the relative silence.

"No. We should wait until someone comes."

"We're on camera, Melody. If they can see us out there, they can see us in here too. We need to get out of here," said Harvey, obscuring his face from the view of the dome-shaped security camera fixed to the ceiling of the train. He stood and pulled Melody with him.

The man's eyes followed his every move as Harvey peered outside the train for signs of a torchlight or approaching rail staff.

The voice of the train driver came over the speakers.

"This is a security announcement. My apologies, ladies and gentlemen. We've been asked to stop here and walk to the next station. If you could please disembark and make your way to the front of the train."

"Just stay with the crowd, Harvey," said Melody. "We haven't done anything wrong."

The other passengers in the carriage stood and shared in the confusion, each of them finding Harvey and Melody staring back at them with guilt written all over their faces.

"Just follow the crowd," said Melody.

But as the passengers made their way towards the open doors at the far end of the carriage, Harvey turned back to Melody, pulling her close to him.

"No," said Harvey, as passengers from the other carriages made their way along the narrow raised footpath that ran along the side of the tunnel. "We need to get away from the cameras, and fast."

"And how do you suppose we do that?" said Melody, as a man reached out to help them down from the carriage. She waved him off. "I'm fine, thank you, sir. I'll wait."

"Follow my lead," said Harvey, keeping his voice low.

He jumped the small gap then turned and reached for Melody to help her across. But she was already beside him. Slowing to let the crowd move ahead, Harvey checked behind him to make sure they were the last in the line. Then he stopped.

"What are you doing?" said Melody. "Keep moving."

But Harvey remained still, pulling them into the side of the tunnel and out of sight.

"We need to stay off the cameras," said Harvey.

"You're not making sense, Harvey," said Melody. "None of this is making sense."

"If he knew I would be in Trafalgar Square, he's probably watching me," said Harvey.

"So?" said Melody. "We need to get out of here."

"No, Melody," said Harvey, catching the faint light in the wetness of her eye. "If he's watching me, if he's planning another attack, I need to be as far away from crowds as possible."

CHAPTER NINE

For the second time that day, a uniformed police officer raised the red and white tape for Reilly and Cole to pass beneath it. Two vans were parked close to the gate at the end of Villiers Street beside the entrance to Embankment tube station, guarded by two armed police wearing protective head gear and breathing apparatuses.

Temporary barriers had been put up by the HART teams to funnel crime scene investigators into a large tent. Both Reilly and Cole entered the tent on the safe zone and emerged in the danger zone, fully clad in hazmat suits and breathing gear.

"This is ridiculous," said Reilly, hearing his own voice muffled by the full face mask. He opened his mouth to continue his complaints. But then two men in hazmats marked with a red cross on their sleeves carried a stretcher towards them from the small park. Parting to allow the paramedics through, Reilly and Cole both caught a glimpse of the man on the stretcher. His green uniform was distinct.

"Did you see that?" said Cole, when the paramedics had passed.

"Early responders," said Reilly, gesturing at two paramedic motor-cycles parked in the danger zone further along the road. "Poor sods didn't stand a chance."

"They must have run right into it," said Cole.

"Are you ready for this, Cole?"

"Let's get in there, sir," she replied.

They turned the corner, stepped through the park's gated entrance and stopped in their tracks.

"Oh my," said Cole.

"Let's let the paramedics do their thing," said Reilly. "We're looking for the device. Note the locations of all cameras and mark the kill zone on a map of the park. Sketch it if you have to. We can't help these people. But if we can find some kind of clue as to who and what this is, we might be able to stop this guy before he strikes again."

"Copy that, sir," said Cole.

She walked off towards the centre of the scene, leaving Reilly standing alone at the edge of the park, staring at the array of bodies that looked as if they had been arranged by a Hollywood set designer. He took a breath and felt his own exhalation on his skin, warm and moist. The next inhale was warm and stale like used air. He blinked away the heat in his eyes and tried to wipe them, but his hand hit the face mask and he dizzied a little. In an instant, his breathing grew faster. It was as if there was no oxygen and he was trapped in a box. He leaned on the park gate and doubled over, forcing himself to breath. But still, the hyperventilating continued.

His hands fumbled at the mask, but the gloves were restricting his movements.

He turned from the park, his hand finding the red plastic barriers that funnelled him into the white tent. But he wasn't even halfway there when he realised he wasn't going to make it. He had to get the mask off. He had to breathe fresh air.

Seeing him stumbling, a member of the HART team ran to his aid.

"Sir, are you okay?" she said.

Reilly stared through the mask, mouth wide open, trying to suck in the air. The woman began to lead him away, tugging at the breathing apparatus to check the valve was opened.

The inside of the tent was dark in comparison to the winter morning sunlight and Reilly's eyes struggled to adjust in time. Still fighting for breath and with the added blurred vision, his panic increased.

"Let me out," he said, in between raising breaths. "Get me out of this thing."

"Sir, calm down," said the lady who had come to his rescue. "Let's get you hosed off."

"No. Just let me out. I need air," he said, as his vision blurred almost in its entirety.

Two strong arms pulled him away and forced him beneath an open shower. The sound of rain against the hazmat material beside his ears added to his confusion and state of panic.

"Thirty seconds, sir, and you'll be out," said a man's voice. "You're nearly there. Just hang on."

But it was too much. First, one knee buckled and another hand supported him. Then the other knee gave way and he slipped from the grasp of his aid to the floor.

Voices, muffled with distance but loud with urgency, span around him. Darkness bore down on him and just a thin trickle of oxygen was extracted from each labouring breath.

Then, like a cool breeze washing across his naked body, his senses numbed.

Darkness closed in.

And there was silence.

CHAPTER TEN

"Stay with him," said Lucas. "Don't let him out of your sight."

"Oh, I don't know if I can do this," replied Herman, his stomach bunching into a knot. "There's too much evil. I can't do it."

"You can't do what, Herman?" said Lucas. "You can't find the man that destroyed your life? Or you can't push a few buttons to save the lives of your family?"

Herman stared at him in the reflection of the computer screen, his face a picture of misery.

"You know I'll do it," said Lucas. "The only reason they're still alive is because of you. Look at what you've done. Look at how far you've come."

Hanging his head with the fatigue and stress from two days of being locked in a tiny apartment, with his captive family and the blood of so many people on his hands, Herman began to weep.

"Oh, stop your crying," said Lucas. "We've got work to do. Where's Harvey Stone?"

"I don't know," said Herman.

"But you have access to every CCTV camera in London, Herman," said Lucas, his voice softened and calming. "You told me you could do this. We can't stop now, dear brother." He raised his hand to the left side of Herman's face and traced the outline of a scar.

"Stop it," said Herman, and pulled his head away.

"We're doing this for you. Remember? We're doing this so you can live, so you can grow, and so your boy can remember his pa as a great man with power and strength, not the dirty little pervert who couldn't keep his hands to himself. Or do you want him to believe the picture the public paints of you?" said Lucas.

"I can't let my boy see me like this. I don't deserve to be a father," said Herman. "Maybe it's best if he-"

"If he what?" snapped Lucas.

Staring into the screen, Herman lost himself in a trail of thought that seemed to lead him by the hand through the images of London and to someplace cold, dark and lonely. It was a safe place, a place away from the taunting boys, the jeering crowds and the look of hate in every eye that jabbed at his very soul with their opinions.

"If he what, Herman?" said Lucas, snapping him back from his safe place.

He looked up and found his brother in the reflection of the screen. He opened his mouth, struggling to form the word, although he knew it and knew how to articulate it. But to speak it was alien. Inhuman.

"Dies?" asked Lucas, prolonging the noise and adding a sense of joy to the rising tail of his public school boy articulation.

There it was.

The word.

"Yes," whispered Herman, his voice more of a breath than a word. A short, sharp exhale followed like some part of his subconscious found a thin slice of humour in his thoughts and forced it through while his consciousness was numbed with the mental imagery. "At least then he wouldn't have to suffer as I have. At least, if he was dead, he wouldn't have to endure the agonising taunts from the boys. He wouldn't be the boy whose father is the pervert. He wouldn't be the boy that causes girls to huddle together when he passes like some contagious monster."

The final sentence fell from Herman's lips, leaving his mouth hanging open in memory of the words.

"At least he would die with the innocence he deserves," finished Herman.

"Snap out of it," said Lucas, his voice loud and his tone sharp. He slammed his hand on the desk to add weight to his command. "In two days' time, you'll be walking the streets with your head held high with your boy by your side. And you know what, Herman? He'll be holding your hand and looking up at his father as he walks beside you, trying to match your step. And he'll be proud, Herman, proud to be your son. He'll feel safe. And you know why? Because his father will be a man who will take care of him. His father will be the type of man who won't let anybody take advantage of him, who won't let anybody hurt him. Is that what you want, my dear Herman?"

The scene in Herman's head softened his expression. He closed his eyes and clung to the thought like a fist grasping at the cold morning fog. And as the last wispy trails of the dream vanished, he opened his eyes to stare at his brother in the reflection of the screen.

"Tell me, dear brother. Is that what you want?" whispered Lucas.

The question danced across Herman's mind between flashes of the dead lying on the cold, hard ground.

"Is that what I want?" he asked, confirming the question as his focus returned to the damp, dark apartment. "Yes. Yes, I want him to feel safe. I want him to hold my hand. I want him to match my steps, to keep pace with me. And yes. I want him to be proud of his father."

"Good," said Lucas, tracing the outline of Herman's ear with his finger. "So let us continue."

"Yes. Yes," said Herman with a new burst of life.

The energy brought a smile to Lucas' face. He opened the small notepad on the desk to the page marked with the lid of their pen.

"Who's next?" asked Lucas. "Look at the list, Herman. Tell me who's next."

A long, unmanaged fingernail trailed a list of names from top to bottom. A tongue eased from between Herman's lips. Then his face hardened as his finger came to a stop.

He looked up at Lucas, who stared back at him through the screen's image of people in white suits carting the dead and dying onto stretchers, but said nothing.

"Good choice, Herman, my dear brother," said Lucas. "Good choice."

CHAPTER ELEVEN

"Follow me," said Harvey, and he ran further into the tunnel, following the other passengers. He stopped and stood flat against the wall when they reached the station and began to file onto the platform. Melody crept up beside him and peered along the tunnel.

"What are we going to do?" said Melody, peering after the small, scared crowd edging their way along the tunnel.

"You're going to follow them," said Harvey. "Mingle with the crowd, get in a taxi, drive one mile then find another. Lose them, whoever it is watching us. Lose them."

"What? No," said Melody. "I'm staying with you."

"Listen," said Harvey. He turned from watching the passengers climb up to the platform to look at Melody. "Whoever this is, he knows where I am. And he's one step ahead. I need to get away."

"Where will you go?" asked Melody.

"I'll find him," said Harvey, and he met her stare. "I'll stop this."

"Harvey, no. That's how trouble finds you, Harvey. Just let the authorities deal with it for once."

"They've done a great job so far, haven't they?" said Harvey. "And what am I supposed to tell them? I used to work for an organised crime family and now I have someone trying to kill me?"

"Do you think it's someone from-"

"I don't know who it is, Melody. I have no idea. All I can do is get out of here and track them down. I can do it. I'll be okay. But if..."

He paused and turned away.

"If what, Harvey?" said Melody.

He sighed.

"If anything happened to you, I don't know what I'd do. You're the only solid thing in my life right now," said Harvey. "If I didn't have you, I'd have nothing."

Melody pulled him in close and hugged him. He felt her swallow and clear her throat.

"I'll make a deal with you," said Melody.

"What's the deal?"

"You get yourself out of here. Stay off the cameras and lose the tail. Then come find me and we tackle this guy together?"

"No. Melody, I-"

"I won't hear another word, Harvey," said Melody, as she pulled her jacket off and tied it around her waist. "If you're not going to the police, if you're doing this alone, then I come with you and that's final."

"And when we find him?" said Harvey.

"We take him to the police," replied Melody. "No guns. No weapons. We do this clean. We said we'd start a new life here. I'm not having it tainted just because you can't go to the police."

The words circled in Harvey's mind like vultures circling a corpse with their wings spread wide, hanging on the breeze. Then they closed their wings and descended to their prey.

"Okay," said Harvey. "Now go."

"Go where?" said Melody, as Harvey walked back into the tunnel.

He turned, took the few steps back towards her and kissed her hard, cupping her face in his hands.

"I'll find you," he said, then slipped into the darkness.

CHAPTER TWELVE

"Sir, can you hear me?" said a voice. It came to him like the voice of a faraway angel, bringing with it a warm breath that quelled the cold grip of his slumber. "Sir?"

A clicking sound, close to his face, moving from side to side.

Reilly opened his eyes to find dark shapes against bright white.

The clicking continued.

"That's it, sir," said the voice. "Take it easy."

The shape focused as if someone was adjusting the lens of a camera. The image brightened to reveal a pair of pretty eyes, soft in heart but with a hardened appearance behind glass.

"Cole?" said Reilly.

"I'm here, sir," replied Cole. "You had a giddy turn. You're okay. But we need a paramedic to check you over. Are you okay with that?"

"A paramedic?" said Reilly, still digesting his circumstance. "Where am I?"

"Villiers Street, sir," said Cole. "We were investigating the-"

"The gas bomber," said Reilly, interrupting her with his recollection.

"That's right, sir. You've been out for a few minutes. Just relax. We've asked one of the paramedics to pop over. He'll be here shortly."

"No," said Reilly, and rolled to his elbow.

"Sir, stay where you are."

"No, Cole. Let me up."

"Sir, you need to relax," said Cole, as a second lady bent to help restrain him.

"Just relax, Mr Reilly," said the woman. "I'm afraid I can't let you leave. We have to have you checked out. This is still a controlled zone and it's HART's jurisdiction." She turned to Cole. "Go get the paramedic. Tell them to hurry."

"No," said Reilly. "I'll wait. I'm okay."

"But, sir," said Cole, torn between the two instructions.

"Let the paramedics deal with the injured. I'm okay. I'll wait," said Reilly.

"I'm afraid I'm going to have to ask you to wear your oxygen mask, sir," said the woman in white. "If you breathed in-"

"I won't be wearing that, I'm afraid," said Reilly.

"But, sir, if you have inhaled the chemicals-"

"If I breathed in the chemicals, I wouldn't be talking to you now. And besides, if I did breathe them in and I'm dying, I won't be spending my dying breaths wearing that bloody thing."

The woman nodded at Cole, who relaxed and returned to Reilly's side.

"Help me sit up, will you, Cole?" said Reilly, as he pulled himself around to lean against a table leg. He nodded once more to the woman, reconfirming his position on the paramedic and the oxygen, and offering thanks for allowing him a little comfort.

"Do you remember what happened, sir?" asked Cole.

"I blacked out. The air. It was constrictive. I felt boxed in," said Reilly, struggling to end the words to say how he'd felt. "I felt like I was suffocating."

"Do you have any history of claustrophobia?" asked the woman, who still lingered nearby.

"No-one likes being trapped," said Reilly.

"But it affects some more than others," replied the woman. "It's nothing to be ashamed of."

"I'm not claustrophobic. It was the mask. It must be faulty or something. There was no air."

The woman in white stared down at him, her lips taut and her smile false. "I'm sure," she said.

Leaving the woman to surmise her own opinion, Reilly turned to Cole. "Did you find anything?" he asked, moving the topic of conversation away from his own weakness.

"A rucksack," she replied, reaching for her bag. "I've asked for the CCTV footage to be sent through while it's taken to the lab. Early inspections show it's a homemade device triggered by a mobile phone."

"How does a phone trigger the release of gas?" asked Cole.

"We can't be specific to this case until the bag has been examined. But typically, an incoming call will initiate the detonator by sending a current through the phone's circuitry, and the explosion will occur when the circuitry powers down, usually when the call goes unanswered. In the past, bombers speed up the process by programming voicemail to kick in after three or five rings. It gives them enough time to get away and avoids somebody intercepting the call."

"So he knows what he's doing then. Do we know what the gas is?" asked Reilly, glancing at the woman. "That might give us a clue."

The woman collected a notepad from a nearby table and flicked back a few pages.

"Early findings are showing it as a chlorine bomb. We found residue on the plants in the bomb's locale. The symptoms support this."

"The symptoms?" said Reilly. "People are dead."

"The symptoms of the survivors, Mr Reilly. We think another toxin has been added to the chlorine to increase its toxicity."

"What are the symptoms?" asked Reilly.

Taking a long breath, as if preparing herself to say the words out loud, the woman closed her notepad and leaned against the table.

"Those who were fortunate enough to survive all have inflamed respiratory systems. They are relying on permanent oxygen feeds. The survivors who were closest to the bomb when it released the gas are experiencing non-cardiogenic pulmonary edemas and may never see the light of day again."

"What's a pulmonary edema?" asked Cole.

"Fluid on the lung, which can be fatal by itself, but when you add the inflamed respiratory systems into the mix, they don't stand a chance," said the woman. She offered Reilly a grave stare. "It's just a matter of time."

"But in the open air, surely the effects are diluted?" said Reilly. "I mean, I can understand how that could be deadly in a confined space, but in the open?"

Nodding in agreement, the woman pushed off from the table and walked across to the front of the tent to stare outside.

"The gas release would be toxic for a few seconds, maybe ten, in these conditions. The wind is fairly strong and constant. But the cloud gas that would have been emitted would have been enough to affect people in a twenty-metre radius."

"So the survivors were all in that radius?" asked Cole, as she tapped on her tablet, scrolling through the images.

"We can assume so. The CCTV footage will give us a clearer picture," said the woman. "The poor souls in the centre of the gas release wouldn't stand a chance. Even if they ran, they would still have inhaled two or three lungfuls."

"And that would be enough?" asked Reilly.

"More than enough," she replied. "The effects would be instant. The body would react to the gas and inflame."

"So they suffocated?"

"The people that died on the scene would have, yes," she replied. "The survivors will die a much slower and more painful death."

A pause followed the statement as each of them processed the information in their own way.

"Sir, I found something. Look at this man and woman. Here," said Cole, turning the tablet to him.

"What's that in the guy's hand?" asked Reilly.

"A mobile phone, sir."

CHAPTER THIRTEEN

"There he is," said Lucas. "Do you see the confidence in his stride, Herman?"

Herman nodded.

"You're going to take him down. You're going to bring him to his knees. And when he's there, fighting for his life, he's going to ask why. He's going to question everything he ever did to deserve such suffering. Say it," said Lucas. "Say his name out loud."

Looking at the list, Herman found the third name down and thought of the misery the man had caused.

"Jasper Charles," said Herman, remembering the man he'd met as a boy and what he'd done.

"It's okay," said Lucas, seeing the memories unfold. "You're getting stronger with each one."

"I want to be there," said Herman. "I want to see it happen. Not on the screen. I want to watch him suffer in real life."

A warm joyous sensation grew from the pit of Lucas' stomach at the words. His top lip rose in a cruel smile, revealing his stained teeth. His tongue emerged to wet his lip then slid back into his mouth.

"Shall we? Shall we go and spectate?" said Lucas. He turned from the computer and stared out of the window, imagining the possibilities. "We could follow him and witness his final moments. How I'd like to stand over his body and remind him of the things he did to you."

"I just want to see from a distance. Far enough to be away from the gas, but close enough to see the look in his eyes."

"Oh, you'll be close," said Lucas. "You'll be close enough to hear his dying breath. Close enough to remind him of the terrible things he did. Tell me, Herman. Where do we find him?"

"He's a manager. In Chelsea. An Italian restaurant. A place called Via Venato."

"Sounds posh," said Lucas.

"It is. They have seafood and fine wines and pastas," said Herman, recalling the online menu.

"Was he hard to find?"

"No. The restaurant has a photo of him on their website."

"So he isn't hiding. He's unashamed," said Lucas. He turned back to the screen. "You'll deliver his surprise to the restaurant where there will be no escape. We'll need the van and paperwork. Delivery notes, you know, the stuff they sign."

"I'll have a clipboard," said Herman, his enthusiasm growing as the plan unfolded. "And a trolley with boxes."

"And a uniform," said Lucas. "That'll throw them off the scent."

"I can find out who their suppliers are and fake some delivery papers and a uniform."

"No. We take the supplier's van. We take their uniform. There can be no mistake. Can you hack their restaurant delivery system?"

"Of course," said Herman, with renewed confidence.

"You are such a talented boy, Herman."

"I'll get into the restaurant's system and find out who their suppliers are," said Herman.

"And then?" said Lucas, brimming with excitement.

"I'll hack the supplier's system and find out when the next delivery is."

"That's the ticket. I can see it now, Herman. Oh, how special will this one be? I can see you standing there while someone signs your papers. I can see him walking through those swinging double doors, full of pride and authority. That's when you do it. That's when you pull the mask to your face and watch him choke," said Lucas, drawing out the last three words, savouring the flavour of his brother's revenge.

The computer screen was split into four CCTV feeds. Every ten seconds, the feeds changed to another four cameras. Millions of people passed by in monochrome. Tourists clung to each other's arms and looked around in wonder at the ancient buildings. Workers hurried by with routine, a daily walk, a daily cycle, a daily drive. Beyond the tourists, workers, bicycles and cars, Lucas found Herman staring at him.

"You can do this, Herman," said Lucas. "You can really do this. It'll be your greatest yet."

"Yes."

"Just think of the beatings, Herman. Think of the shame, the humiliation and the torturous nights he put you through when you were just a boy."

"Stop," said Herman, hanging his head. "I'll do it."

"And when you do," said Lucas, "be sure to look him in the eye. Be sure to remind him who you are and wait for that moment. That moment when his pupils dilate. When his mouth opens just a fraction and the recognition sets in."

"And it'll be too late," said Herman.

"There'll be no escape," said Lucas.

"But what about Stone?"

"Leave Stone to me. We'll save the best for last," said Lucas. He stood from the old swivel chair beside the computer desk and strode to the window. "You're still learning. You're still growing. And with each name on that list, you grow a little more. But mark my words,

Herman, Stone is out there somewhere. He has to surface soon. And when he does, we'll find him. You can track the phone we gave him."

"What if he throws the phone?" asked Herman.

"Oh, he won't. He's got nowhere left to hide."

"Do you think he'll come after us?"

"Almost certainly, dear Herman," said Lucas, and placed his hand against the cold glass window. "We've woken the beast."

CHAPTER FOURTEEN

The tunnel was devoid of sounds, save for the scurrying of rats, distant murmurings of trains being disembarked, and their passengers stumbling confusedly along the dark corridor.

Step by step, Harvey sought the raised platform, running his hand along the damp, brick wall to his right for guidance. The empty platform ahead offered little in the way of refuge, only bright lights, the smell of grime and the noise of a rolling drinks can being pushed along by the incessant breeze.

From the darkness, Harvey studied the platform. The exit tunnel, which was shiny with white tiles, snaked out of sight towards the station and escalators. Two CCTV cameras faced the exit from the platform.

Beside the exit was a set of double doors marked as staff only by a sign branded with the London Underground logo. Breaking them open would create attention.

Harvey ran the scenarios through his head. Whoever it was that was out to get him would find Melody and assume Harvey was close by. By the time they checked the surrounding stations, Harvey would be out and far away from the cameras.

He climbed onto the platform, tried the double doors and found them locked, as expected. So he took the exit tunnel.

The long bends seemed endless, masking any sign of the end. But the shiny white tiles echoed every sound, providing Harvey's only clue as to what lay ahead. The click of a door being closed echoed along the corridor. A rattle of keys followed and then came the sound of a man clearing his throat.

Harvey slowed his pace, listening for the man's approach, but he heard nothing.

He stopped.

Heels clicked on the tiled floor, growing louder.

A man's whistle, tuneful and relaxed.

Then a shadow on the curved wall began to grow like some monstrous demon rising up from the floor. With nowhere to turn but back the way he came, Harvey pressed himself against the wall. But the shadow grew larger still from the floor up the walls and across the arched ceiling.

And then a boot stepped into view.

It stopped.

Another rattle of keys and then the opening of another door with an audible squeak of dry hinges that played backwards as the door closed behind the man with the solid touch of heavy wood on wood.

Harvey moved forwards with slow, cautious steps, rounding the bend as close to the wall as he could. He found the door on his right and peered around the corner. An armed policeman travelled up the escalators with his arms resting on his weapon, rocking from his toes to his heels, in what Harvey could only assume to be a method of maintaining the circulation in his feet. The policeman disappeared from view, blocking the only exit known to Harvey.

Moving back to the door, Harvey listened for movement inside, but heard nothing.

The door handle, a brass knob that appeared to be several decades old, rattled at his touch and the squeak of the hinges seemed louder than before. Inside, he found a service passageway with electrical panels fixed to the white tiles at head height. A series of switches that Harvey presumed to be lights were fixed beside the inside of the door.

He closed the door behind him, easing it into place with practiced silence.

A man cleared his throat somewhere close. He was in the left passage, Harvey deduced with his head cocked to one side. The whistling began, allowing Harvey to place the distance. He was close by and tinkering with something. Harvey pictured the scene as the sounds came to him.

A small screw being placed on a metal container. Then another.

A metal panel being removed.

The whistling stopped. Concentration.

Harvey opened the panel on the wall to the right. A series of electrical breakers were sitting in four rows of fifteen. Each of them was marked with a small label that Harvey presumed to be electrical circuits. At the bottom of the panel was a single breaker, larger than the rest.

Harvey placed his finger beneath it, but hesitated, considering a plan that was formulating in his mind.

"Here, what are you doing in here?" said the old man, stepping from the service passage as he tucked a screwdriver into the breast pocket of his coveralls and pushed his glasses onto the bridge of his nose. "You aren't supposed to be in here. What are you doing?"

Harvey gauged the man to be in his late fifties. He wore a few days' growth and his wrinkled face was tanned with age beneath a flock of smooth, grey hair.

Placing a single index finger to his lips, Harvey gestured for the man to be quiet, conscious of the armed guard outside.

"Don't tell me to be-"

Harvey flicked the switch.

In an instant, the small passageway was plunged into total darkness. A hum of ventilation that Harvey hadn't previously registered fell silent.

"What have you done?" said the man, and stepped towards Harvey. His footsteps were loud enough for Harvey to guess his distance, reach out, place one arm around the man's neck, and cover his mouth with the other.

A green light above the doorway flicked once then shone a dim ghostly light over the room.

"I don't want to hurt you, old man," said Harvey. "But I will if I have to. Do you understand?"

A feeble nod beneath Harvey's grip.

"I just hit the main breaker. Is the station in darkness?"

Harvey loosened his hand.

"Just the emergency lighting, son," said the man.

"Good. Do you have duct tape?"

There was a pause. Then the man nodded and tapped Harvey's arm with the roll from his tool belt.

"Pull a piece off about eight inches long."

The man's eyes widened, but Harvey offered no indication of emotion through his blank stare. He took the length of tape from the man.

"I'm going to remove my hand. If you call out, you die. If you struggle, you die. Do you understand?"

The old man nodded once more.

"Give me the roll of tape."

He did as he was told.

"Put your hands behind your back."

"It's you, isn't it?" said the old man, as he did as instructed. "You're the one they're looking for."

Harvey pulled his arms tight then loosened them a little, to allow the old man some comfort, before wrapping a long length of tape around his wrists. Then Harvey pulled the tape across the man's mouth, tugging to make sure it was tight.

"Can you breathe?" asked Harvey.

The old man nodded.

"Are you in pain?" asked Harvey.

The man shook his head. The movement was barely discernible in the dim, green light.

"Last question," said Harvey, and released the tape from the man's mouth. "I need to get out of the station without being seen. Where the nearest exit?"

"Go up the escalators and turn right," said the old man. "Go through the double doors and you'll see a fire escape. It brings you out onto the side street."

"And the CCTV?"

"You just killed the lights to the entire station. CCTV won't pick you up until you hit daylight at the top of the escalators."

"Do you understand what I'll do if you're lying?"

There was a pause. Then the old man nodded.

"If anybody asks?" said Harvey.

"Just go, son. This place will be swarming with police in a few minutes," said the old man. "I didn't see your face."

"I'm sorry I had to do this," said Harvey, as he pulled the tape back across the man's mouth.

The old man appeared to be unafraid. He stared up at Harvey and watched as he opened the door, took a glance outside, and then ran.

CHAPTER FIFTEEN

"The faces on the left were all victims of the Jubilee Gardens bomb, sir," said Cole, presenting a series of printed photographs that had been stuck to a magnetic glass wall.

"The deceased?" asked Reilly, sipping at his coffee with one hand. His other hand turned a coin over in his pocket. It was his method of keeping his shaky hand away from the inquisitive Cole.

"The dead and dying, sir," replied Cole. "Any one of them could have been the target, if indeed there was a target."

"So the faces on the right-hand side are the victims of the Victoria Embankment Park bomb?"

"Precisely, sir," said Cole. "We're looking for any links between any of the people on the left with any of the people on the right."

"A common factor?" said Reilly, nodding his approval. He gestured at a large TV screen that was mounted on a trolley to one side of the rows of faces. A video had been paused on the optimal shot of the man with the phone. His features were clear and cold. "What about the man with the phone?"

"Tech are running facial recognition now," said Cole. "He's not wanted by the police for anything. So they're running him against the database."

"And the girl he was with?"

"Same, sir," replied Cole. "Although her scarf covers most of her face. We should have answers soon. Until then, I'm working on the victims, starting with those closest to the bomb."

"Good," said Reilly. "So who do we have? Is there anybody that might have enemies?"

"These four here," said Cole, indicating the top row of four faces, "were closest to the Jubilee Gardens bomb. This lady's name was Rose Clare, a hairdresser from Lambeth."

"What was she doing there?" asked Reilly.

"We don't know yet. But she was found lying beside this guy," said Cole, moving to the next photo. "Patrick Gervais. An associate partner in an accountancy firm across the street from where the bomb went off."

"A couple meeting for lunch?" offered Reilly.

"Likely, sir. They were both unmarried," said Cole, moving to the next photo of a red-headed man with tattoos that crawled from his chest to his neck and a thick beard. "Anthony Robinson. Art director for a web design firm. His office was two minutes away from the park. His wife and child have been informed."

Reilly shook his head, inhaled long and slow, and gestured for Cole to move onto the last image.

"Jason McMillan. A mechanic from Essex. Visiting the London Eye with his wife and two children and had just left them to get a drink from a nearby shop when the gas took him down."

The pause was enough to not have to ask the question Reilly was avoiding.

"His children escaped without harm," said Cole.

"And his wife?"

"She died a few hours ago, sir," said Cole, her tone low and quiet. "She ran into the gas cloud to help her husband before the gas had fully dispersed. Her body just gave up."

A thick knot sat at the back of Reilly's throat. He swallowed, but still, it remained.

"Who does this, Cole?" asked Reilly. He stopped turning the coin and swapped the coffee to his other hand, aware that Cole had seen the shake. "We're not going to find the answer here in time to stop him striking again."

"There may be a clue, sir."

"There will be a clue," said Reilly. "But we don't have time. He's out there preparing to hit us while we're down."

"How do you know it's a he?" said Cole.

"I don't. I'm stereotyping. Not many women could do that to children," said Reilly.

"And how do you know it's one person and not a group of them?"

Reilly sighed. "I don't. I'm going with my gut."

"Based on experience?"

Reilly nodded. "It's a homemade device using chemicals available on the open market. No terrorist group has claimed the attacks and only a handful of people have lost their lives."

"A handful of people, sir?" said Cole, her face twisting with incomprehension. "We have forty bodies on our hands."

"I know it sounds callous, Cole," said Reilly. "But how many did we have after seven-seven? How many did we have when the IRA blew up the city and the docklands?"

"More. But still-"

"And each of those bombs were followed up with a call to the prime minister taking ownership for the blasts."

It was clear to Reilly that Cole wanted to hate him for his remarks. But her eyes softened, betraying her emotions.

"What we have here is a vendetta, Cole. You're right. There's a clue in those names and faces and we need someone on it. But not you. Right now, we need to focus on that man with the phone, and whoever the hell he's with."

"Her face isn't shown. She's wrapped up in a scarf, sir. I think we'll have better luck finding him on the database."

"What about the phone?" said Reilly. "A call was being made. Maybe it triggered the bomb? Can we trace it?"

"Not after the fact, sir," said Cole. "Besides, it's probably a burner."

"And where does he run to?"

"Embankment underground station," said Cole. She lifted her laptop to control the video on the large TV and began to talk Reilly through their escape. "They take the westbound train, but they don't get far before the security protocol stops the trains and evacuates the passengers."

"After that?"

"They disappear."

"What's the next station after Embankment?"

"Westminster, sir," said Cole. "But they didn't show up. Same with the next two stations."

"Show me the girl again," said Reilly.

A few mouse clicks later, Cole had the picture of the girl up on the screen. She slowed the video to frame by frame then paused it on the clearest shot. The video was monochrome and pixelated.

"Now show me the passengers evacuating from Westminster station," said Reilly.

A few moments later, a video of Westminster station exit appeared on the screen. Passengers hurried through the doors, checking behind them. People clutched their bags and one woman with two children held them both close, trying to flag a taxi in competition with the other passengers.

"She's not here, sir," said Cole, selecting a new video. "Here's the platform where the passengers come out of the tunnel."

Sipping at his coffee, Reilly sat back on the edge of the desk and folded his shaking hand beneath his arm. Just as Cole opened her mouth to say something, he saw her.

"There," he said, standing and moving to the screen. Reilly pointed to the last passenger to climb from the tunnel. "This girl. This is her."

"Sir, she doesn't match-"

"It's her. Play it back."

The video reversed then played back frame by frame.

"Wait for it," said Reilly. "Here she comes. Look at her. Why is she only wearing a t-shirt in the middle of December? And look how she glances back for just a fraction of a second."

"You're right, sir," said Cole.

"Find me that girl," said Reilly. He tossed his polystyrene cup into the waste bin, walked across to the TV screen and jabbed at the girl's face. "We've got thirty-six hours before millions of people descend on London, and she knows something."

CHAPTER SIXTEEN

A row of warehouses backed onto a wide, concrete opening that was dotted with trucks and articulated lorries. Forklift trucks ferried goods from the lorries to the warehouses, while the drivers leaned against their rigs. Men in various coloured uniforms wheeled trolley loads of boxes to the smaller trucks.

"There's our truck," said Lucas, staring through the windscreen of their little car. "The green one with the back doors open."

"How are you going to do it?" said Herman. "We don't have to kill him, do we?"

"You leave the truck to me, dear brother," replied Lucas. "You need to focus on the job at hand. Run me through your plan."

"My plan?" said Herman. "I don't really have one."

"You know where to park the truck?"

"In the loading bay behind the restaurant."

"And then what will you do?"

Catching sight of the glint in his brother's eye in the rear-view mirror of their car, Herman looked at the truck three hundred yards away and lowered his voice, as if reciting a dream.

"I open the back of the truck, check the delivery notes for the right boxes-"

"That's important," said Lucas. "They'll be expecting the right boxes and they'll know what they look like. We don't want to cause suspicion."

"Right," said Herman.

"Carry on," said Lucas. "I'll play Jasper. Come on. It'll be fun."

"I wheel the boxes into the back door of the restaurant."

"Can I help you there?" said Lucas in a mock Italian accent.

"I've got a delivery," said Herman.

"You've got a delivery?" replied Lucas. "And what is it a delivery of?"

"Erm," said Herman, "I'd need to check the delivery notes. I don't really know."

"Fail," said Lucas, his voice loud in the confined space of the car. "You just annoyed the man. He's running a kitchen. He doesn't have time to mess around."

"But how do I know what I'm delivering?"

"You check the paperwork beforehand, Herman," said Lucas. "Let's switch. I'll be you, and you can play soon-to-be-dead Jasper."

Turning in his seat to see his own performance in the rear-view mirror, Lucas cleared his throat.

"Can I help you there?" said Herman. His Italian accent was weak and his voice trembled.

"Are you Jasper?" said Lucas, putting on his best London accent whilst flicking through a make-believe clipboard.

"Yes," said Herman.

"I've got three boxes of napkins, two boxes of sea salt, and a particularly nice crate of Vermentino. A gift from the boss," said Lucas, and winked in the mirror.

"A gift from the boss?" replied Herman.

"A new year's gift for his favourite customer," said Lucas, slotting into the role with ease. "He sends his regards, of course."

"Oh," said Herman, unable to think of a response suitable for the role play.

"If you just want to sign here, Jasper," said Lucas, and he imitated handing over the clipboard. "I'll show you a bottle."

He stopped and his London accent fell away to his usual harsh, monotone voice.

"That's when you do it," said Lucas.

"That's when I pull the mask out?" asked Herman.

"And deploy the gas," said Lucas. "He won't stand a chance. You'll stand over him while he suffocates and you'll get to see the panic in his eyes. You'll get to smell his fear, Herman."

"But what if I get it wrong?" said Herman. "What if I mess it up and he suspects something is wrong?"

"You won't, and he won't," said Lucas.

"And the wine. Where will I get the wine?"

"There is no wine, Herman," said Lucas, struggling to contain his impatience.

"But you said there was a box of wine."

"The box of wine is the gas, dummy," said Lucas. "There is no wine. But we need a reason to be delivering an extra box, don't we?"

"Right," said Herman. "I see."

The driver of the green truck slammed the door and pulled a wide U-turn across the concrete.

"But what about Stone?" asked Herman.

Lucas studied the driver as he passed then watched the truck fade into the distance.

"You leave Stone to me, my dear little brother," said Lucas. "You leave him to me."

CHAPTER SEVENTEEN

A kick to the handle of the fire doors sent them slamming back into the walls and a blast of cold air greeted Harvey in an instant. He scanned the area for police, but found only a side street devoid of people save for two taxis waiting for a fare near the top of the road.

He opened the rear door for the first cab and slid inside.

"Elephant and Castle," said Harvey, pulling the door closed as sirens began to wail nearby.

"I hope you're not in a rush, mate," said the driver, as he pulled out onto Westminster Bridge.

"Is traffic busy?" asked Harvey, feigning ignorance.

"Been another one of them gas bombs," said the driver. "Bloody nutters, they are."

"Is it the same guy?" asked Harvey.

"It must be," replied the driver. "They hit Jubilee Gardens the other day and now they've hit the little park outside Embankment station. Bleeding transport police have shut all the trains down. I heard it on the news."

"I'm surprised you're still working," said Harvey. "Isn't it safer to get out of town?"

"I am, mate. I was waiting for a fair to take me out of the city. The least I can do is help someone get home."

"Right," said Harvey, as another police car shot past in the opposite direction. "Do you think they'll catch this guy before New Year's?"

"I don't know, mate," said the driver. "I mean, how do you catch someone like that? It's sick, is what it is. Whoever is doing this must be an absolute nutcase. It's lucky most people are off work for the holidays. It could have been a lot worse."

"I agree," said Harvey, and peered out of the window. The traffic moved in one direction like a mass exodus lumbering from danger in a slow moving crawl to safety. "Have they said how many people have died?"

"Two dozen in the first bomb. Plus I heard there's more in hospital, but the chances of survival are pretty slim," said the driver. He shook his head and tutted. "What a world, eh?"

Harvey didn't reply.

"Drop me here," he said, when the taxi emerged from a back street close to Elephant and Castle junction. He pulled a twenty from his pocket, slid it through the gap in the glass and waited for the door lock to click off.

"Take care, mate," said the driver, as Harvey stepped out.

"You too," said Harvey, and closed the door.

The taxi drove off, leaving Harvey standing at the kerb watching the flow of traffic. A few miles from the attack, the people were less hurried, but anxious to get home. In less than two minutes, a second cab trundled along the bus lane. Harvey flagged him down.

"Where you going, mate?" asked the driver through his open window. "I'm only heading out of town."

"Clapham," said Harvey.

"That's good enough for me," replied the driver, and released the rear door.

The driver muttered under his breath at the other road users, leaving Harvey free to drop the innocent charade. He pulled the phone from his pocket, hesitated, and then hit the power button.

A few seconds later, the phone found a signal but sat dormant in Harvey's hand. He opened the messages, but found none. The list of recent calls contained only one number.

The taxi driver meandered through the back streets, crossed main roads and avoided the traffic the way only black cab drivers know how. They arrived on Clapham High Street, where Harvey tapped the glass partition.

"Anywhere here will be fine," he said, and slid another twenty beneath the glass.

The cold bite of the wind hit him as soon as he was out and he watched the taxi join the ranks of traffic.

Harvey walked to a side street to get out of the wind and noise of the main road. He found a doorway, which felt warm in comparison to outside, then pulled the phone again from his pocket.

He hit the button to bring up the recent calls, selected the only number that showed, and then hit the green button and waited for the ring tone to begin.

"Harvey Stone," said a timid voice. "Is it really you?"

CHAPTER EIGHTEEN

"We've got her, sir," said Cole. Her breathing sounded heavy over the phone connection. "Facial recognition gave us everything we need. Tech guys found her on social media and another search found that she's just rented a house in Wimbledon."

"Where are you now?" said Reilly, holding the phone with one hand, while his other hand struggled to tip a single tablet from a pill bottle.

"Out running, sir. I'll be back in an hour."

"You're running at a time like this?"

"It helps relieve tension, sir. You should come with me one of these days. You'll feel better for it."

A single pill fell onto Reilly's desk. He snapped the bottle closed.

"I'd only slow you down, Cole," said Reilly. "Besides, I have my own ways of dealing with tension. Whatever works for you."

"Can I speak freely, sir?"

Reilly closed his eyes and readied himself for another round of unwanted advice. "Of course," he said, and dropped the pill into his mouth.

"The answer isn't in a bottle," said Cole. "I know it's not my place, but-"

"That's right, Cole," said Reilly.

He paused, refraining from saying more and deepening the rift between them.

"Whatever works for you, sir," said Cole.

"So what's your plan?" said Reilly, moving the subject on. He raised the tumbler of whiskey to his nose, inhaled the sweet fumes, and then took a sip to wash the pill down his gullet.

"I'm assembling a team, sir. We've got the go ahead for a raid," replied Cole. "Armed support in case it gets ugly. Air support in case they run."

"They?" said Reilly. "You have them both?"

"We don't have a name for the male, sir, but we do have a face. She's pictured with him-"

"Don't tell me. On social media?"

"Yes, sir."

"Who'd have thought the answers to our problems would be lying amongst pictures of cats and people's dinners?"

"It's a digital world, sir," said Cole. The sound of her voice changed as if she accepted the she wasn't escaping the call and had slowed to a walk. "There's no escaping it now."

"For better or worse, Cole," said Reilly. "Talk to me about surveillance."

"I've got two teams already in place, sir. She's home alone."

"So you're hoping the man with no name returns in time? What if the surveillance scares him off?" said Reilly. "He might be watching from a distance for all we know."

"I said the same, sir," said Cole. "But word from the top is that they want a face to put out on the media before New Year's Eve. If this affects the New Year's celebrations, the damage to the UK reputation could be irreparable."

"That's a big risk," said Reilly. "We could lose this guy for good.

He'd still be free to do it again. The consequences could be far worse than a damaged security reputation."

"True," said Cole.

"No doubt you have something up your sleeve?"

"The thinking behind it is that it'll draw him out," said Cole. "But we need more resources."

"We need every camera in the city manned until he shows up. But we won't get that," said Reilly. "I'll find out what resources we can get. As a minimum, I'll ask for a mile radius around the two attack sites."

"A mile? Sir, that's thousands of cameras and we can't be sure the next attack will be in the same area."

"No, but he's struck the same area twice. He could be targeting one particular person."

"I had the same thought," said Cole. "He might have missed his target the first time and lined up a second."

"In which case, he might never show his face again," said Reilly. "Or he could be a nutter. Plain and simple. An angry soul who wants the world to see how powerful he is."

"Statistically there's a target, sir," said Cole. "And that could break down into a religion, a company, a political opinion. Or it could be an individual."

"We haven't found any links between the victims yet," said Reilly. "So let's assume he has a target. We'll need to know if any of the victims had enemies, if they were up to no good or mixed up in something."

"That will take weeks, sir," said Cole. "New Year's Eve is tonight."

"That's my point, Cole," said Reilly. "We need to plan for the worst. I want every camera in a square mile radius around the attack sites manned. I want the girl taken underground. No public announcements. And I want a team digging up every bit of dirt on the victims. This is a war, Cole, and I don't intend on losing."

"No public announcements, sir?" said Cole. "The PM wants a

face to show, a public enemy captured. If we don't have that, we could have bigger problems."

"Do we have a deadline?"

"Six p.m.," said Cole. "Six hours before the celebrations."

"By my watch, that gives us four hours to break her," said Reilly, and tipped the remainder of his scotch into his mouth.

CHAPTER NINETEEN

"Harvey Stone. Is it really you?"

Harvey didn't reply.

"I've been thinking about you," said Herman, holding the phone to his ear with his shoulder while he pulled the car into a parking spot a few hundred feet behind the green truck. "I've been thinking about you a lot."

Harvey didn't reply.

"Talk to me, Harvey, please," said Herman. "You're trying to place my voice, aren't you? You're trawling through that catalogue of obscenities in your mind, searching for a face to put to the voice. There's so much I want to say."

"Well, you found me. So say it," Harvey replied.

"Do you know how long I've been thinking about you, Harvey?" said Herman, tracing the outline of the steering wheel with his left hand, picturing Harvey's face.

Further up the street, the driver of the truck opened the rear doors, pulled out a trolley and checked his paperwork against the boxes inside.

"Longer than I've been thinking about you," said Harvey. "You obviously want something. I'm not playing games. This call is over."

"No, no, no," said Herman. "Are you there?"

"I'm here," said Harvey, after a pause.

"If you could see the dreams I've had. Just you and me. Alone with nobody to get in our way. Nobody's attention to contend with," said Herman. "Nobody to hear the screams."

"Or I could just carry on with my life, ditch this phone and forget all about you," said Harvey.

A long blast of a car horn sounded in the distance and wind rasped through the phone's speaker.

"Could you, Harvey?" said Herman. "We've been planning this for a long time. You're outside right now, aren't you? You can't go home. Am I right? I'm right, aren't I?"

Harvey didn't reply.

"Let me guess. You made it out of the city and you're somewhere familiar. Somewhere where you know the back streets. But you can't show your face in case we find you."

"Are you going to tell me what you want?"

"You haven't even asked me my name yet, Harvey," said Herman. "Do you even care who I am and what you put us through?"

"It doesn't matter who you are. In fact, it's better if I don't know."

"Oh, we're so alike. We have so much in common. I'd love to get to know the real Harvey Stone. I'm sure you'd grow to enjoy my company."

"We have nothing in common. You tried to kill me once and failed," said Harvey. "I never fail."

"Hmmm, don't be so sure," said Herman, as the driver of the truck emerged from a small restaurant in South London. "It's a shame. I'd love to talk to you. I'd love to see inside your mind."

"So let's meet," said Harvey.

"I thought you'd never ask," replied Herman, glancing in the rear-view mirror and finding his brother's approving nod. "How about lunch? Somewhere warm. Or are you as cold-blooded as they say you are, Harvey Stone?"

"Name the place," said Harvey.

"Via Venato. Fulham. One hour," said Herman, as he pushed open the driver's door of his little car.

"Fulham High Street?" said Harvey.

"That's right. We made a reservation under the name of Harvey Stone," said Herman, smiling at his brother's genius. "We thought it best if we meet in public. I hope you don't mind, but you do have a bit of a reputation."

"And after that?" said Harvey. "Are you going to tell me what this is all about?"

"I'll explain it all over lunch," said Herman. "I have to go. I..."

"What?" said Harvey.

"I can't wait to see you, Harvey Stone."

He hit the red button to disconnect the call and pocketed the phone.

"Good work, Herman," said Lucas, as he slipped his Taser from his pocket. "That wasn't too hard, was it?"

"I remember him so clearly, Lucas," said Herman.

"Hold that thought, dear brother," said Lucas. "Just hold that thought."

The driver was just loading his little trolley onto the back of the truck and was about to jump down to the ground and close the rear doors when Lucas approached.

"Excuse me, sir," said Lucas in his finest broken English with a strong flavour of Germanic. The driver looked up and waited for Lucas to reach him. Lucas smiled the friendly smile of a helpless tourist, retrieved a folded map from his pocket and began to point. "I am trying to find the train station. I wonder if you may help me."

CHAPTER TWENTY

Harvey climbed from the third taxi he'd been in that day and closed the door. Three teenagers wearing skin-tight jeans, sweaters with sleeves that covered their hands and dark make-up around their eyes strolled past. None of them glanced at Harvey, each lost in the music that played through their headphones.

A father walked with his two children and their little dog, hurrying as if they were late for something. The children wore hats pulled down over their ears and thick coats buttoned up to their chins.

Steel shutters were pulled down over a few shop fronts, but most outlets were open, taking advantage of the holiday season. A clothes store advertising a fifty percent discount across their entire range had drawn the attention of two women who were looking through the window. One wore a black furry hat with her long blonde hair hanging over a tight leather jacket. The other wore a pair of knee high boots, tight jeans and was letting the cold wind keep her dark, curly hair from her face.

With bus lanes on either side of the road, there was no place for parked cars. Harvey studied the face of every man he saw. An old man with a walking stick coughed into a handkerchief then resumed his slow amble. A tall man in a suit, talking into his phone, stood by the kerb. He finished the call and flagged the next taxi before disappearing.

An image of the man Harvey had seen in the park flashed to his mind. A slither of a face shrouded by the green hood. Distinctive eyes, pale like an albino, but lined with fatigue or memories.

Or suffering?

The face matched no man in view so he stepped over to a phone box. The exterior remained the classic red London phone box that was known across the world. But the inside had been upgraded with the latest technology.

The coin slot received a one pound coin. Harvey tapped the number from memory then waited for the connection to be made and the ring tone to begin. It lasted five rings then silenced.

"It's me," said Harvey.

"Are you safe?"

"I can't talk," he said. "I just wanted to know you're okay."

"I'm fine," said Melody. "I'm worried about you. Just who is this-"

"I made contact," said Harvey. "It's best if that's all you know."

"What are you going to do?"

"I'm going to finish this," said Harvey. "Stay low."

He replaced the handset and hung his head to rest on his arm, picturing Melody in their new home. She'd be cleaning the kitchen, seeking a distraction. The more she thought about what she'd seen and what might happen, the harder she would scrub, venting her anger and frustration through the grime.

A laughing child ran past the phone box, breaking Harvey's thoughts, then stopped and waited for his father to catch up. Nearly ten shops down from the phone box on the far side of the road, Harvey could see the cream signboard with the words Via Venato. It was printed in black, scripted font as if somebody had handwritten the name of the restaurant on a napkin and declared it the company logo.

He checked the time then glanced at the people walking by.

No green hood.

No slither of face.

No pale eyes.

Keeping to his side of the road, Harvey made his way past the restaurant, scanning the customers inside with two swift, casual glances, as a shopper might. The restaurant appeared to be laid out similarly to every other restaurant Harvey had dined in. A selection of two and four seated tables stood against the windows with four seaters occupying the centre space and a handful of family-sized booths against the rear wall. A pair of double doors led to the kitchen out back. The restaurant was served by three waiters.

Continuing past the restaurant, Harvey ran the image of the lunchtime customers through his mind. An elderly couple had taken a two seater table by the window. Four men filled one of the four seaters, but were sitting casually with glasses of wine like old friends catching up over the holidays. A family were seated in one booth: husband, wife, and two children, one boy, one girl.

The perfect family.

Harvey crossed the street and doubled back, keeping to the road-side to maintain his view through the restaurant windows. Then, with a glance back over his shoulder, he entered the building and let the door close behind him.

The chat of the restaurant hit him like the friendly hug of a long lost friend, and a waiter approached, his eyebrows raised as if he was waiting for Harvey to talk.

"You have a reservation, perhaps, sir?"

"Harvey Stone," said Harvey, keeping his voice low.

"Ah, yes, Mr Stone. This way please," said the waiter, taking charge with his soft Italian accent. He pulled out a chair from beneath a two seater table in the centre of the window and waited as Harvey checked the room, the double doors, and then sat.

"May I take your coat, sir?" asked the waiter.

Harvey shook his head, met the stare of the elderly woman sitting across from him with her husband, and then averted his eyes.

Offering Harvey a small, cardboard menu, the waiter smiled and informed him that the soup of the day was pumpkin sage with Italian ham.

"Will you be dining alone?" said the waiter.

The question sounded easy to answer. But uncertainty clouded Harvey's thoughts. He opened his mouth to speak but hesitated.

Everything was wrong.

"Sir?" said the waiter, prompting him for a response.

Harvey stared at him, trying to match the face to the slice in his mind. But the waiter's eyes were dark and wide with almost sickeningly smooth skin surrounding them.

"Is everything okay, sir?" said the waiter. The repeated question attracted the stare of the two children in the booth to Harvey's right.

"I'll be dining alone," said Harvey, lowering his head and watching the inquisitive children through his peripheral vision as they grew bored and returned their attention to their food.

A rush of cold air swept across the floor as if a door had been opened at the back of the restaurant. He checked the room again. The customers. The elderly couple. The friends.

The perfect family.

He stood, knocking his chair back.

"Is everything okay, sir?" asked the waiter, as Harvey met the stares of each customer.

The hush of chatter fell to silence.

"What's he doing?" asked the little girl who had been watching him. Her question caused her parents to turn and stare.

The banging of a door in the kitchen and the murmur of voices.

"Sir?" said the waiter.

The silence continued.

The gap of light beneath the double doors flashed bright white, accompanied by a loud metallic crack.

Harvey felt his eyes widen and heart stop. He raised a chair above his head, preparing to hurl it through the broad glass window as the doors burst open and a man wearing kitchen whites staggered through, clutching his throat.

Harvey hesitated. Behind the chef stood the shape of a man holding a mask to his face. Even through the protective glass and thick yellow smoke, Harvey saw two pale eyes staring directly back at him.

CHAPTER TWENTY-ONE

"Sir, tech intercepted a call to Mills' house," said Cole, as she stepped into Reilly's office, sliding her phone into the pocket of her jacket. "No names. But it's him."

"Do you have a transcript of the dialogue?" said Reilly, glancing at the door in a silent gesture for Cole to close it.

"The call was short. Less than a minute," said Cole, as she pulled a sheet of paper from the blue folder in her hand and slid it onto his desk. She perched on the edge, clutching the folder to her chest, and waited for Reilly to read the transcript of the call.

"Seven lines," said Reilly. "Less than fifty words."

"I said it was short," said Cole.

He studied the dialogue once more.

"'It's me', he said," said Reilly. "That's confirmation he's not in the house."

"I've got the raid team on standby," said Cole.

"Good. Let's not blow this," said Reilly. "She asked him, 'Are you safe?'"

"Sentiment?" asked Cole.

Reilly nodded. "The social media photos of them together

support that. And in the fourth line, Mills states she's worried about him."

"'I can't talk'," said Cole, reading the next line out loud. "That suggests he knows he's being watched. But we've only just worked out who Mills is. So who's watching him?"

"It's the next line that intrigues me," said Reilly, picking up the sheet of paper from his desk and sitting back in his chair. "'I made contact. It's best if that's all you know'. He's protecting her."

"From us? Or from whoever else is watching him?"

"'I'm going to finish this. Stay low'," said Reilly. He turned in his swivel chair to look out of the window. The River Thames flowed past beneath the office and the London skyline appeared black and featureless against the blanket of grey sky. "He's going to finish it."

"What's he going to finish?" said Cole.

"And when did it start?" said Reilly.

"You're suggesting the first gas bomb wasn't the beginning of this?"

"Potentially," said Reilly, closing his eyes to picture the man and what his motives might be.

"He's going to finish it. Another gas bomb?" said Cole.

"Maybe the two gas attacks were failed attempts," said Reilly.

"Failed attempts on a single target?"

"What if he made the attacks public to disguise who the target is?"

"Because he knows we'd make the connection."

"Does that mean the victims of the first attacks were unnecessary?"

"They were just masking the motive."

"But this time he's going to try harder?" said Reilly. "The language he uses in the transcript, it's definitive."

"A bigger bomb?"

"More casualties."

"A bigger audience."

"New Year's Eve," said Reilly, dropping the sheet of paper to his desk and staring up at Cole. "Keep the surveillance on Mills. It sounds like he won't return until he's done what he set out to do. We need to move in and take her now. She's the only one who knows who this guy is, and the only way we're going to stop this is by knowing who he is and what his motives are. Who is she anyway? What's her background?"

"There's not a lot of information in the usual places," said Cole. "In fact, there's a huge gap in her whereabouts."

"How big is the gap?"

"Five years."

"What did she do before the gap?"

"Do you really want to know?"

Reilly allowed his expression to answer the question.

"Police," said Cole.

It was a response Reilly wasn't ready for. He sat forward, leaning his elbows on his desk and burying his face in his hands. "In London?" he asked.

"Yes, sir," replied Cole. "Exemplary career too."

"But then she vanished?"

"She didn't vanish, but her career did. There's no record of what she did. Just a P45 to close off her employment, and then nothing."

Pushing himself to his feet, Reilly sighed and strode to the window. "London seems so peaceful from here," he said. "So much history. So many secrets."

"Sir?" said Cole. "Are you feeling okay?"

"What did you do before you wound up here in counter terrorism, Cole?"

"Major crimes, sir."

"And before that?"

"I worked my way up through investigative support, sir," she replied. "Why?"

"Investigative support?" said Reilly. "Are you sure about that?"

"Do you have a problem with my methodology, sir?"

"Not your methodology, Cole."

"So what then?"

"When you ran a search for Mills, what did you do exactly?" said

Reilly, letting his eyes trace the outline of the dark roofs against the grey sky.

"It was a standard search, sir," replied Cole. "I followed protocol."

"So break protocol."

"How?"

"Start by searching in the cracks. I'll get you clearance."

"The cracks, sir?"

"I would hazard a guess, Cole," said Reilly, "that Miss Mills was an exemplary police officer so she worked her way through the ranks. And finished up where?"

"Organised crime, sir," said Cole.

Reilly nodded his approval. "From there, she didn't just disappear, Cole," he said. "Nobody just disappears. The paper trail is harder to follow, sure. But nobody disappears."

"Are you saying she stayed in the force, sir?"

"Sharp girl," said Reilly.

"I don't understand. Why would her records stop?"

Turning from the window, Reilly stepped across to her and held out his hand. Cole handed him the blue folder, trying to gauge where he was going with his thoughts. He lowered his voice to a murmur, and leaned close enough for Cole to smell stale alcohol masked by peppermints.

"Let's just say that there are certain necessary operations the force doesn't associate itself with and therefore doesn't recognise."

"Dark ops, sir?" said Cole. "I wouldn't even know where to start searching for that."

"That's good because you wouldn't find anything," said Reilly.

"What if she's still in the force? What if she's working undercover?"

"You would have had a tap on your shoulder if you got too close, Cole," said Reilly. "A polite word in your ear to drop your investigations on Miss Mills."

"So if she's no longer active..."

"If she's no longer active, Cole," said Reilly, letting the folder fall to his desk with a slap, "it means she's super smart, highly trained, and she's somehow involved in the case."

A pause, as both Cole and Reilly processed the idea of what and who they might be up against, was broken by the door being pushed open.

"Sir," said Vaughn, a young officer, keen and green, who had popped his head into Reilly's office.

Reilly held Cole's eyes for a moment longer then turned his head to face Vaughn.

"I'm sorry to trouble you, sir. But there's been another attack."

CHAPTER TWENTY-TWO

Thick, yellow smoke hung in the air like a poisoned fog. The few screams of kitchen staff faded to gargled chokes, but even the sound of the dying soon faded.

All that remained was the sight of Harvey Stone.

Hands tugged at Herman's legs, pleading for help with waning strength. Bloodshot eyes stared up at him. They were wide, not with fear, but with the knowledge that death was seconds away.

And then recognition.

A hand released his leg and pointed up at Herman in disbelief, but the look weakened as Jasper Charles failed to inhale his last breath of air through his swollen throat and bleeding lungs.

The hand on Herman's leg relaxed and Jasper fell to the floor. Herman stared in wonder as the man tensed then twitched as if something inside him fought the battle to the end.

Bending to a crouch, Herman laid his hand on Jasper's head and met his eyes, feeling pity and sorrow.

Lucas' words played through Herman's mind in a whisper.

"It had to be," said Herman.

Jasper blinked, releasing tears that ran from his dying body, carving flesh-coloured lines in the yellow dust that coated his skin.

"You know what you did to me," said Herman, his voice soft, not cruel. He found sympathy for the man who had broken him. He also saw desaturated images of Jasper as a young man and Herman as a mere boy with a naivety that begged for guidance and confidence, not the sick games Jasper had played.

In Herman's mind, the two sat beneath the bridge in the local park. A small river flowed by and incessant rain dulled the view outside, cocooning them in that space. It was as if, beneath the bridge, they were safe, and to step outside through the mist of rain, they would enter a new world where their secrets could never be told.

But Herman's secrets were safe with Jasper. That's what he'd said as they sat on the cold, loose stones, reassured by Jasper's wandering hands.

"You shouldn't worry about what your parents will say," Jasper had said. "They treat you like a child. But look, look how much of a man you've become."

Herman had pushed him away as society had told him he should. But the rain outside and Jasper's persistence made him stay. Besides, he hadn't wanted to leave. Jasper had made him feel like a man, like a grown-up, and had shown him what grown-ups do, there beneath that bridge.

"You did this to me," said Herman, smoothing the hair on Jasper's head. "You made me who I am. You made me into a monster."

But Jasper's eyes no longer flicked in wonder and question at Herman's. They stared to nowhere, no longer instruments of sight but matter, matter that would perish, decompose and leave nothing but a stain on the earth.

"A stain on the earth," said Herman, out loud to himself. "That's what you made me. The things I did to those poor boys was all because of you. The things they shamed me for, the lives I ruined, was all because of you."

The sound of a door closing nearby broke Herman's thoughts,

sending his memories scampering away to hide in the cold, dark corner where he kept the visions of the terrible things he'd done.

Safe. So that nobody could take them away.

He stood and glanced around at the bodies on the floor, bodies in white aprons, checkered pants, hair nets and chef hats.

Out front, a few cautious people peered inside. No longer hidden by the thick, yellow smoke, Herman stepped back to the door, remembering Lucas' words about the escape. As the first sounds of sirens approached, one man stared back at him, his eyes boring into him like daggers. Memories of a rainy night, of pain, of his own suffering.

But Lucas' whispered voice banished the thoughts back to the darkness.

"Run."

CHAPTER TWENTY-THREE

The steel legs of the chair burst through the pane of glass. The cool wind outside sucked at the yellow gas. Harvey tore the cloths from empty tables, sending cutlery, empty glasses and condiments crashing to the ground, and tossed them at the family of four.

"Cover your mouths and get out," said Harvey.

Two of the four friends remained seated and open-mouthed, too shocked to move. The other two edged towards the door, undecided as to the right thing to do and aghast at the kitchen worker who lay crumpled on the floor, twitching at their feet.

But it was too late for them. The yellow haze had found them and the first of them dropped to his knees, wheezing, wide-eyed and clutching the nearest table.

"Leave him and get out," said Harvey, and pulled the father of the family to his feet. "Get your family out and don't breathe until you're clear."

The frightened father gave him a grateful but unsure look, but Harvey hurried him along, pulling each family member from the booth, then shoving them to the door. With his shirt pulled over his face, Harvey ran to the old couple. The old man sat with his eyes closed, fighting for his last breath. His arms lay across the table, clutching those of his wife, who sat unmoving and staring back at him as the last of her life left her body.

"Move," shouted Harvey at the two surviving friends who were helping the family through the door. The last of them stopped to glance back at his two dying friends one more time. "Now."

Ripping a cloth from a table for himself, Harvey stepped over the waiter to the broken window. He sucked in a lungful of fresh air, glanced once at the gathering crowd and heard the approaching sirens. Harvey covered his face, turned, and walked through the double doors that were held open with the bodies of the kitchen staff. He saw the back door slam shut.

In an instant, Harvey gave chase.

Bursting through the rear doors, he tossed the table cloth to the ground and scanned the alleyway, just catching sight of the man he'd seen through the fog disappearing around a corner.

The world rushed by in a blur as Harvey's arms pumped harder than ever before, pushed on by the adrenaline that surged through his body. He turned the corner, taking it wide to maintain his speed, then ran into the road to avoid a group of people who spanned the width of the pavement. Behind them in the distance, the man ran across the street heading for a bright green railway bridge that crossed the road. Beside the bridge was a car tyre shop, its shutters down, closed for the holidays. As Harvey followed, the man leaped onto the bins outside the tyre shop.

Harvey closed the gap. He was seconds behind. As the man pulled himself onto the roof of the tyre shop, Harvey slammed into the wall beneath him, reaching for his ankle and missing by inches.

A police car screeched to a halt behind him. Harvey glanced back, saw the officers climbing out of the car, then looked up to see the man's leg disappearing over the wall.

"Armed police," called the officer. "Stop or we'll shoot."

Time stopped for the briefest of moments. Melody's words sounded clear in Harvey's mind.

"That's how trouble finds you, Harvey," she'd said.

Harvey glanced back once more at the officers who were closing in, took a breath of fresh air, then pulled himself onto the roof and leaped across to the train tracks.

One hundred yards to Harvey's right, the man, who had ditched the uniform he'd been wearing and pulled his hood up over his head, ran along the trackside, turning for a nervous quick look back.

Large, grey stones lined the ground around the sleepers and tracks, and barely an inch of wall remained that wasn't adorned with graffiti. Then two hands appeared at the wall beside Harvey and the muzzle of a rifle followed.

Slamming his boot into the police officer's fingers, Harvey then leaped over and shoved him off the wall. His partner raised his weapon and aimed, but it was too late. Harvey was already on the heels of the man in the hood.

The stones crunched underfoot. They slipped and twisted at Harvey's ankles. Ahead, the hood was suffering the same problems. The chase slowed but continued. The tracks to Harvey's left gave off a soft hum and buzz of electricity, signifying an approaching train, warning him away from the tracks. Ahead, the hood ran on, doubling his efforts to escape Harvey.

But then he stopped. He turned back to face Harvey and, for a moment, he pulled his hood away, revealing the white skin of his face. And as the approaching train rushed past Harvey, the hood covered his face, and ran across the tracks.

Glimpses of the man climbing the wall and disappearing from sight through the momentary gaps between the train's undercarriages put the chase to an end. The train finished passing and Harvey stepped across the tracks, all urgency gone.

The man was nowhere to be seen.

Instead, the thumps of an approaching helicopter brought with it new dangers.

Behind him, several police officers and dogs had climbed the wall and were on his heels.

With nowhere to hide, Harvey continued to run along the tracks. Behind him, the barking of the dogs grew louder and the constant thumping of the helicopter's rotor blades seemed to add to the chaos. It wasn't until Harvey reached the bridge that spanned the River Thames that he saw his escape blocked by more police coming the other way.

He turned in time to see the handlers letting the dogs free. There were two dogs, both jumping on the spot, eager to run Harvey down.

The helicopter burst into view overhead, banked, and came around, level with Harvey. It yawed, bringing its opening side door to face Harvey. A man appeared, raising a rifle to his shoulder.

With the dogs closing in behind him, the police in front blocking his escape, and the sniper in the chopper taking aim, Harvey took his only option.

He jumped into the murky brown water that rushed past below him.

CHAPTER TWENTY-FOUR

The same officer that had lifted the red and white tape at Jubilee Gardens let Reilly and Cole through to the scene on Fulham High Street. Although he demonstrated professionalism, his face conveyed a deep-rooted anger.

"Do you see those cameras up there, Cole? Have the tech guys send the footage through as soon as possible. I want to see anyone who entered the building in the past forty-eight hours."

"I'm on it, sir," said Cole, pulling her phone from her pocket and moving to one side.

Three ambulances were parked at the side of the road by the rear doors and EMTs in green coveralls tended to two small children and two adults who looked to be their parents. The second ambulance had a young man wrapped in a red blanket, his face buried in his hands. His friend was standing close by, leaning against the vehicle, rolling a lit cigarette between his fingers, blank faced and red eyed.

An officer, deep in discussion with two others, glanced up and saw Reilly. Then he tapped the man in front of him and muttered something inaudible. The man raised his head, dropped some paperwork to his side and inhaled, his chest expanding as he prepared to greet Reilly.

"Connor," said Reilly, keeping his tone business-like and offering his hand. "Were you first on the scene again?"

"One of my unit was," said Connor, nodding at the officer who had let Reilly through. He shook Reilly's hand in what could be assumed as comradeship over manners, rank or jurisdiction.

"How does it look?" asked Reilly, taking a moment to gather his senses and get a lay of the land before entering.

A red mist formed over the whites of Connor's eyes. He turned away and cleared his throat. Giving Connor the time he needed to compose himself, Reilly studied the front of the building. Uniforms had taped off the area and blocked the street. A helicopter thundered overhead.

"Some guy ran from the scene," said Connor, seeing Reilly's eyes follow the chopper until it disappeared over the buildings. "They chased him onto the train tracks about five hundred yards that way." He gestured with his paperwork hand to indicate the direction.

"Did they get him?" asked Reilly, knowing the answer would be negative.

"No," said Connor, tight lipped and shaking his head. "Mad bastard jumped in the river. I got the news about two minutes before you showed up. It's a shame. I'd have loved to have got my hands on him."

"He's dead?" said Reilly, feeling a squeeze on his gut relax for a glorious second. "I presume we have river support out there?"

"It's three degrees," said Connor. "If the fall didn't kill him, the cold will. No doubt, we'll find his body downstream in a day or two and you'll be able to close the case off. Another roaring success."

Connor's bitter statement caught Reilly off-guard. He opened his mouth to say something, but paused.

"Sorry, Reilly," said Connor. "I shouldn't take it out on you."

"Don't apologise," replied Reilly. "This isn't easy for any of us. Thanks for doing what you've done here."

"We'll keep the area cordoned off. CSI are en-route. Just get in there and do what you need to do so these people can get back to their lives. With any luck, this is the last of it."

"What should I expect in there?" asked Reilly.

"Twelve dead," said Connor. "It's not pretty."

"And the device?"

"In a box in the kitchen. One of my guys did a pass through before he realised it was the gas bomber."

"So the gas has cleared?"

"You should still suit up, Reilly," said Connor. "Don't take any chances."

Nodding, Reilly made to leave. He glanced across at Cole, who had her hand on the shoulder of the man with the cigarette. The family at the first ambulance were all huddled together beneath blankets and the HART team were constructing a white tent on the pavement.

"Connor," said Reilly, stopping the man as he walked away. "Do me a favour and keep me posted on the body in the river. I'll have my hands tied up in there. I could do with the help."

"I will do," said Connor, and nodded his appreciation.

A senior member of HART crossed his arms and waved Reilly away as he approached.

"Five minutes, sir," he said. "It's a no go until then."

Diverting, Reilly walked past Cole, who needed no interruption, and stopped at the nose of the foremost ambulance. He leaned against the bodywork and stared into the broken window, wondering how it had all gone down. A couple held hands across a table but slumped in their chairs as if they held each other up. The doors to the kitchen were held open, but offered him little view of what was inside.

"Penny for them," said Cole, the heels of her boots growing louder as she approached.

Reilly turned his head away.

"How long until we suit up?" she asked, tapping on her tablet and swiping through various applications.

"HART says five minutes," replied Reilly. "Did you get the footage?"

"I got everything we need," said Cole, and handed him the tablet. A frame had been taken from the video and enhanced. Using his finger and thumb to expand the image, Reilly centred on a man's face as he entered the restaurant.

"Black leather jacket," said Reilly.

"Same boots. Same pants," said Cole. But her eyes were on Reilly's shaking hand, not the image on the tablet.

"And the same cold expression," finished Reilly, handing the tablet back to Cole. He pushed off the ambulance and stuffed his hand into his pocket. "Let's go."

"Sir, we need to suit up," said Cole, calling after him.

He stopped but didn't turn.

"We're not suiting up," said Reilly, and watched as she caught up with him. He waited until she was by his side and lowered his voice. "We're not going in."

"But, sir, it's the crime scene."

"And I'll tell you what we'll find. We'll find twelve dead faces that will haunt the rest of our lives. We'll see carnage and chaos, and we'll see panic and fear. But you know what we won't find?"

"The bomber?"

"Get the teams standing by, Cole," said Reilly, giving the restaurant one last glance. "We're taking Mills underground."

CHAPTER TWENTY-FIVE

Cold hands found hard rocks and numb fingers sank into soft mud.

The current tugged at Harvey's heavy legs, pulling him along for the ride, until his boots found purchase on the debris that lay beneath the treacherous water.

Unknown strength pulled him free then subsided and dropped him like the river might let trash fall to its bed.

He rolled to one side, felt the bitter wind against his aching body and, for a moment, let the darkness creep in. Long, black fingers muted his mind of anything but the warm arms of death, shrouding his vision and clouding memories that might sway his inner strength.

But there was one memory the darkness was unable to conceal.

One memory of two pale eyes beckoned him further. The memory gave strength to his legs and carried him through the mud to where a small wooden jetty, dark and stained by the river, reached into the water and provided shelter from the wind.

The tide lapped at the mud, boats cruised past, and with nothing but his muddied clothes for warmth and the growing night for cover, he climbed the concrete wall and dropped to the riverside footpath below, grateful for the holidays and sparsity of people. A small patch of grass nearby offered him a single tree with thick bushes at its roots, a place for him to wring his shirt, tip his boots and bang the mud from his cargo pants.

But the biting cold found him and sank its teeth into his flesh. With fingers trembling from the cold, he buttoned his pants, and his numb fingers tied his sodden boot laces.

He breathed into his hands, covering his face to bring some feeling back. Then, making sure nobody was in sight, he jogged on the spot, flexing his freezing feet and rigid joints before heading towards the streets in the distance.

A helicopter circled someplace far off, a street corner played host to a group of teenagers, and a car with four young men inside was parked nearby. The unmistakable thud of bass was clear in the early evening. A man leaned into the driver's window then the music stopped, and the boys on the corner silenced as Harvey grew near. Heads turned to watch him approach.

An electric window rolled down, releasing a thin cloud of smoke from the car and the tang of marijuana into the air.

"You got a problem, mate?" said the driver, his face masked by his hood and the shadows.

"Whose car is this?" asked Harvey.

"It's my car. And it's my street. So you best be on your toes, if you know what's good for you."

"I need to use it," said Harvey, checking the street left and right, but finding nothing but the street lights and lit houses.

"You what, mate?" said the driver. "Did you hear this guy, boys? Fool thinks he can walk up to me in my own street and take my car." He turned back to Harvey. "You best be on your way, fool. This is my street and I don't remember saying you could be in it."

"I didn't see a sign," said Harvey.

"Why am I going to give you my car, fool?" said the guy.

"Because you're selling drugs. You're probably carrying a knife and you probably have a record. You act tough, but deep down you know you wouldn't last two days in prison. If you were as tough as you say you are, you would be out of the car right now. But you're not. You're sitting in it because you're scared. So you have two choices."

"Two choices? Is that right, mate?"

"First choice. Give me the car, walk away and don't look back."

The four men began to laugh, and a joint was passed from the back seat to the driver, who took a long pull and eyed Harvey as he sucked in the thick smoke.

"Second choice," continued Harvey. "Stay in the car and I take it from you."

A siren in the distance grew closer then faded as it passed on the main road.

"You're not taking nothing, fool," said the driver.

"You've got three seconds before I make the choice for you. Leave the keys in the ignition," said Harvey.

"Fool, you have no idea who I am," said the driver, and his three friends began to chime in.

"Three," said Harvey.

"You stink, mate," called one from the back, inciting laughter from the foursome.

"Yeah, go back to the swamp, Swampy."

"Two," said Harvey, rolling his neck from side to side and waiting for the satisfying click from each side.

"Boy, you better be on your way and get off my street," said the driver, as the window began to wind up. His voice lowered with bravado but the fear was evident. "I'm not even wasting my time with you anymore."

"One," said Harvey, as the window closed fully.

The heel of his boot smashed through the glass and connected with the driver's face. As Harvey withdrew his leg, he leaned in and pulled the guy from the car. The driver dropped to the ground and scampered away, his voice high, panicked and embarrassed.

"You don't know who you're messing with, fool," he said, as he scurried backwards away from Harvey on his hands and feet.

Leaning into the car, Harvey addressed the other three young men, who were all sitting with their mouths hanging open, aghast at what they'd seen.

"Are you guys coming with me?" said Harvey. "Or are you getting out?"

In an instant, door handles clicked and the three men piled out, backing away from the car as if it was contagious, leaving Harvey free to climb in, engage first gear, and pull away.

He found the main road, recognised the area as Bermondsey, and made his way towards South West London, opening the windows to let out the smell of the joint.

In the centre console, a welcome surprise was waiting for him: a mobile phone in a shiny, plastic case, made to look as if it was gold-plated. Steering with his knees, Harvey popped out the SIM card and tossed it out the open window. He pulled the bomber's phone from his pocket and took out the SIM card, slotting it into the new device. The old, water-logged phone smashed on the street behind him as he joined the South Circular Road and settled in for the ride.

He was just five minutes from his destination when the new phone began to play a rap song. The only number stored on the SIM card flashed up on the screen. Harvey hit the green button, pictured those pale eyes, and waited for the timid voice to follow.

"Are you ready to play a little game, Mr Stone?"

CHAPTER TWENTY-SIX

"All units standby," said Cole into the radio, as Reilly hit the accelerator and spun the wheels. "Mobile one, give me an update."

"No movement at the front," came the reply from mobile one, an unmarked van parked four doors down from the rented house. "But she's home. Lights are on and off."

"Is there any audio?" asked Cole.

"Not a peep," said mobile one.

"Mobile two, what have you got?" said Cole, using one hand to steady herself against the dashboard as Reilly navigated a series of parked cars on a tight street.

"Nothing worth talking about," came the reply. "A few lights turned on and off as she moved from room to room. But nothing out back."

"Good. We're fifteen minutes out. I need armed support covering all exits, and let's see if we can get some eyes in the sky."

"Copy that," said mobile two. "Switching to channel three."

"Where's mobile two located?" asked Reilly.

"In the house behind," said Cole, adjusting the radio to the broadcast channel and turning the volume down to quieten the sudden burst of activity. "The house is up for rent and we gave the agent a good deal on a short-term basis."

"Are you serious?" said Reilly, flicking his head to see her then turning back to the road. "What was the deal?"

"Give us the house for free or we'll report him for renting to illegals," replied Cole, and offered Reilly a smile. "The badge helped."

"It usually does."

"The house is an end plot. We've got mobile one covering the front and side, with mobile two at the back. Nobody has been in or out and what audio we've managed to get hasn't picked up a thing."

"Are you doubting your decision, Cole?"

"We need to be sure, sir," she replied.

"When it comes to terrorists, the rules are different. You have to understand that."

"Who are you referring to here?"

"I'm referring to them all, Cole," said Reilly. "Race, colour, religion, none of it matters. A terrorist is a terrorist. We're not dealing with drug dealers or petty thieves here. They need to be stopped as soon as the evidence is there, not a moment before, and not a moment after. Twice now, we've seen this guy at the scene of the crime and twice he's got away. This girl knows something."

"There're procedures, sir," said Cole.

"And see where your procedure will get you," said Reilly. "You'll need twenty-four hours just to get an answer from her."

"I thought the rules of engagement were different with CTU?"

"The rules are different, but the top brass is the same. In twenty-four hours' time, she'd have said nothing and you'd have the chief leaning on you to get an answer or let her go, worrying about a court case. That's not happening, Cole. Not with this one. I've seen too many bodies these past two days to let this go."

"He's probably dead anyway," said Cole.

"And how's that going to come across on national TV?" said Reilly, dropping into third gear to take a corner. "We failed to catch the man that brought panic, pain and misery to our nation's capital.

But it's okay. We think he might be dead." He shook his head and undertook a car hogging the outside lane. "That's not happening, Cole. I want to know who he is or was. I want to know what all this is about. And I want to be able to stand in front of those cameras and make damn sure those people are safe."

"So you're taking her underground?" said Cole.

Reilly answered with his silence.

"And I'm supposed to go along with it, am I?" said Cole. "I'm supposed to risk my career because you don't want to tell people the truth. You'd rather break all the rules-"

Reilly slammed the brakes, dipped the clutch and eased the car to the kerbside, to the annoyance of the drivers behind him. He leaned across Cole and pulled the door handle. Then he pushed the door open.

"There it is," said Reilly. "There's your ticket out of this. I'm doing it my way and I'm getting results. If you're not okay with that, I won't judge. But I can't let you stop me."

"Sir-"

"We've spoken enough. If you're in, say so and we'll get this done. If you're not, get out. Call a cab. Expense it, if you like. But do not stand in my way."

The two locked stares and several car horns sounded. A driver passed by, glaring out of his open window, and hurled abuse at Reilly, who returned his attention to Cole.

She unclipped her seatbelt and was about to speak when her radio crackled into life.

"DS Cole, come back," said the voice.

Cole held Reilly's stare until he nodded for her to answer the radio.

"This is Cole, go ahead, dispatch," she replied.

"Uniforms picked up a man in his twenties in Bermondsey for possession."

"What does that have to do with the gas bomber?" said Cole, and lowered the radio to her lap.

"He said he had his car stolen from him," came the reply.

"What does he want? Time off?" said Cole.

"No, ma'am," came the reply. "The suspect reported the thief was a man in a black leather jacket, cargo pants and black boots who stank like the river. Thought you'd like to know, ma'am. The suspect is heading west on the south side."

Cole slammed the door, hit the dash switch for the blues, and pulled her seatbelt on as Reilly floored the accelerator and the screaming siren cut a path in the traffic ahead.

CHAPTER TWENTY-SEVEN

"I'm not into games," said Harvey.

"I think you'll find this particular game intoxicating," said Herman, running his hand along a hose that connected three small gas tanks to a small compressor. "I call it 'catch a killer'. What do you think? Think it'll catch on?"

"I think you're insane," said Harvey. "I think you're in above your head and you're scared."

"No. You're wrong," said Herman. "We're strong now. Stronger than ever."

"That makes two of us," said Harvey.

"Well then, now that we're all warmed up, it's your move. What are you going to do?"

Harvey didn't reply.

"You're wondering what your options are."

"You're weak," said Harvey. "I can hear it in your voice."

"No. You don't talk," said Herman. "Let me remind you who the boss is now. You had your turn. You took everything. And now it's my turn."

"So tell me what my options are then," said Harvey. "If you're the boss, show me."

"Option one," said Herman. "Save the pretty girl. Oh, and we must congratulate you. She's very pretty."

"She can take care of herself," said Harvey. "I doubt she's afraid of you."

"That might be the case," said Herman, sitting down in front of the computer screen. "But it's not me she should be afraid of. You're about to lose your only ally. Then you'll be all on your own, just like I was. Do you remember?"

"What's option two?" said Harvey.

"I can see you now," said Herman, struggling to control a fit of childish giggles. "I can see you in my mind's eye. You're sitting in the dark while every policeman in the city is looking for you. It's just a matter of time before they find you. But you don't care, do you? No. You're too strong for that. You're waiting for me to talk. A monologue perhaps? Well, how's this for you, Harv? You can sit there in the dark, giving my voice the freedom it needs to trigger a memory. Something to place my face. Something to complete the triangle. You know me. You recognise me. My name is on the tip of your tongue. All you have to do is reach out and say it."

He stopped and pictured Harvey with his eyes closed.

"Option two," said Herman, softening his voice, luring Harvey to him. "Forfeit the game and spend the rest of your life behind bars."

"I'm not playing games."

"Oh, but you are, Harvey. Don't you see? We've spent a long time devising this game. And we'll play it whether you like it or not. Five long years, Harvey, and every second of that time, we thought about you. We thought about what you might do. We thought about every twist and turn. And we thought about you, Harvey Stone, suffering for all those people you judged. Now it's your turn to be judged."

"What am I being judged for?" asked Harvey.

"Oh, that's a good question," said Herman, as he stood from his chair and pushed open the bedroom door, stopping at the threshold.

Two eyes flicked open in the darkness and stared up at him from the bed at the far side of the room. "But if I told you that, the game would be too easy, and I'm not ready for that just yet. In twenty-four hours, millions of people will be flocking to the city. You have until then to solve the clues. You see, Harvey, while I pondered my misgivings, staring at the walls, I made myself a list. And guess who's on it?"

"I'm not biting," said Harvey. "You want me. You come and get me."

"It began as a list of six. But now there's only three. And when we get to one, it'll just be you and me."

"What do you want me to do? Rhymes aren't my thing," said Harvey.

"We want you to die, of course," said Herman. "We want you to suffer as we have. We want you to beg for your life, cry for mercy, and rain forgiveness on all the lives you have taken."

"I'm not the begging type," said Harvey.

"Then Harvey Stone will be responsible for London's worst atrocity in history. You'll never walk free again. You'll be hunted until the day you die." Herman paused. "Do you remember us, Harvey? Or were there so many that our faces blend into one?" he said, biting his lower lip. "I hope you can remember me. I do so want to see you die."

"So why not tell me who you are now and be done with it?" said Harvey.

"Time," said Herman. "The timing has to be perfect."

"So what now?" said Harvey, after a pause.

"Do you want a clue?" said Herman. "Find the place where long grass grows, between three trees and then you'll know."

Herman hit the red button to disconnect the call and dropped the phone to his side, taking a deep breath to ease the adrenaline that raced through his bloodstream.

"You did good, dear brother," said Lucas. "You're growing stronger."

He stepped over to the bed and brushed Martina's hair from her face, ignoring the muffled objections. She stared up at him with all the murky hatred she could muster, her breath forcing the tape in and out of her mouth.

"Your time is coming, my dear," said Lucas. "Your beloved Herman is growing strong, and soon, all this will be a distant memory."

CHAPTER TWENTY-EIGHT

Killing the lights as Harvey turned into his street, he pulled the car into the first space he found, using the handbrake to slow to a stop to avoid the rear brake lights glowing red. He killed the engine, let his head fall back to the rest, and gathered his thoughts.

The conversation played over in his mind as he committed the words to memory. One sentence in particular played over and over, coming back to him clearly in that monotone voice.

"But it's not me she should be afraid of."

The street was still. Too still.

The scene of the bomb in the park played back in his mind. The hood. The chase. The park.

The camera.

He'd looked up at it.

And Melody.

The scene played back once more.

Trafalgar Square.

The photos Melody had taken.

The two of them together.

On social media.

The chase along the train tracks. It was Harvey they were after and Melody was the key to finding him.

They'd found her from the photos and were ready to strike.

He studied the street once more. It was early evening. The roads were quiet. Parked cars lined the kerb, BMW's and Mercedes, a sign of the area's affluence. Three hundred yards along the street, a single white van was parked between Melody's little sports car and an SUV.

A flicker of doubt stirred inside Harvey's gut.

He climbed from the car and entered the network of alleyways that ran behind each of the streets offering residents a rear entry to their property. He slowed to a walk when he neared the house and, keeping to the shadows, peered over the wall.

A light flicked on at the back of their house. Melody passed by the window. She stopped, held her phone up, and then dropped her hand to her side.

Disappointment or frustration?

The empty house behind was in darkness, a black stain on the street while the neighbouring houses glowed with the lives of families staying home in the warm before the New Year's celebration.

Harvey studied the empty house. The top rear windows offered little view inside. But just as he turned away, he caught a tiny flash of light.

A reflection on the window maybe?

Or a camera lens turning to scan the darkness and monitoring the rear of the house?

Harvey looked closer.

Once more, light flashed as the street lamp caught the end of the lens. He imagined the operative scanning the area with the camera on a tripod.

Seconds passed as Harvey stared up at the window from the shadows of the alley.

The flash of light again.

He began to count.

He focused on the window, nothing but the window.

Twelve seconds, and the light flashed once more.

He scaled the wall and dropped down to the soft grass below.

Ten, eleven, twelve.

He worked his way along the side fence, keeping to the thick hedgerow.

Ten, eleven, twelve.

He dropped to the ground and rolled beneath the hedge.

Ten, eleven, twelve.

He closed the distance to the back door of the house and flattened himself against the wall.

Nine, ten, eleven, twelve.

He forced the back door with the heel of his boot and slipped inside.

Only the rhythmic thud of his pulse in his ears sounded, and the warmth of the house found his damp clothes. The lights downstairs were off so Harvey made his way into the lounge and used the bay window's wide field of view to find the van parked along the street. The rear doors had been fitted with blacked-out windows, as had the side of the van that faced the house.

Using the sides of the staircase to avoid making a noise, Harvey crept up the stairs. A slice of bright light shone beneath the door of the rear bedroom. All other rooms were in darkness.

He placed one foot on the hallway carpet at the top of the stairs, stepped across and put his ear against the door.

Nothing.

Knowing the back bedroom would be monitored by the cameras in the empty house, Harvey stepped away from the door just as a fist came out of the darkness.

With one hand, he caught the arm, twisted it, and pulled it up tight behind Melody's back, placing his free hand over her mouth and pulling her back close into his body.

"Shhh," he whispered, and felt her body relax when she realised he wasn't an intruder.

Harvey released his grip, motioning for them to go into the bathroom. He kept the lights off and ran the shower, using the noise to mask their whispers.

"What's going on?" Melody asked.

"The house is being watched," said Harvey, listening for any changes in sounds outside.

"What?" Her face screwed up in disbelief. "He knows where you live?"

"It's not him that's watching," said Harvey, putting his finger to his lips to keep her voice low.

"So who..." said Melody, then stopped as the realisation hit her. "No."

Harvey nodded. "There's an unmarked police van outside and a crew in the run down house behind."

"What do they want?" she said, glancing through the doorway to the front of the house. "We haven't done anything."

"They have us on camera running from the scene," said Harvey.

"We can explain that," hissed Melody. "We can turn this around."

"They also have me running from the restaurant in Fulham."

Her eyes widened, glowing in the dark. "What were you doing there?"

"I told you I'm going to stop this."

"Harvey," said Melody, a horrified expression creasing her perfect skin, "if they think you're the gas bomber, it won't be the police outside. It'll be special operations. Counter-terrorism maybe. And they won't be taking us to a nice police station for some gentle questioning. These guys don't mess around. They can make us disappear if they really have to. Just give yourself up. We can get you out of this."

"I can't. He's got something planned."

"I told you to let the authorities deal with it."

"By the time they realise it wasn't me, it'll be too late."

"Too late for what?"

"New Year's Eve," said Harvey. "I don't know what, but he's planning something."

"Planning what?" said Melody.

But Harvey just shook his head in response, unable to convey his whirling thoughts into a single intelligible sentence.

"What does he want?" asked Melody. "Is he trying to kill you?"

"Eventually," said Harvey. "It'll be slow and painful."

"So why the bombs?"

"He's got a list. The bombs weren't meant for me. He's working his way through a list of people. It began as a list of six. But now there's only three. And when we get to one, it'll just be you and me," said Harvey, reciting the words he'd committed to memory.

"He's killing everyone who ever wronged him?" said Melody, her brilliant mind digesting the information. "What if the bombs were designed to kill more than just the intended victim? What if the victims could all be linked to him and by killing multiple people, he could cover that link?"

"It's possible," said Harvey, as a loud crack of splintering wood came from downstairs.

They both spun to face the bathroom door.

"Come with me," hissed Harvey, as he reached for the window.

"No. You go," said Melody, and turned towards the hallway to peer outside as heavy boots stomped into the house downstairs. She stepped to the window, reached up and kissed him hard. "Find him and stop him. I'll do everything I can to help."

Harvey opened the window wide and climbed onto the ledge as the heavy boots banged up the stairs and men began to shout for Melody to get down on the ground. She glanced up at him as she dropped to her knees, her hands raised in compliance.

Harvey jumped to the ground below.

CHAPTER TWENTY-NINE

"Cuff her," said Reilly, as he reached the top of the stairs and gave Mills a long, hard stare. She stared back as if to ask why he was wasting her time.

"All clear, sir," said an armed uniform, as he appeared in the doorway to the bedroom cradling his rifle.

"No sign of him?" asked Reilly.

"He's not here," replied the officer.

"I want this place swept for explosives and gas, any sign at all that he's involved," said Reilly. He turned to Mills as the officer began to instruct his team. "Where is he? Where's your man?"

But Mills remained silent, replying with only a cold, hard stare.

"I'll find him, and when I do, he'll be in a whole new world of hurt."

Still, Mills remained silent, kneeling on the bathroom floor. Reilly flicked his eyes around the bathroom from the shower to the bath, and then to the open window.

"It's a bit cold to have the window open in the middle of winter, isn't it?" said Reilly.

Mills looked away to one side then returned her stare.

"Lock the place down. One mile radius," said Reilly, speaking to the officer standing in the hallway behind him. He continued to stare into Mills' very beautiful eyes then turned to find the officer still standing there. "Now. Roadblocks, air support and an officer on every street. He's close and he's on foot."

He stepped past Mills into the bathroom and leaned out of the open window, feeling the cool air on his face. Below him, the side street was bare, but the main road to the front of the house was a hive of activity. Spinning blue lights flashed across the rows of houses, curtains twitched and curious neighbours were standing at their garden gates, wondering what was disrupting their idyllic neighbourhood.

There was no sign of the bomber.

Reilly giddied as if his head had been rocked from side to side. He held onto the window ledge, feeling his slick, sweaty hands slide on the PVC.

"There's nothing here, sir," said Cole.

Her voice sounded distant as nausea took hold. Leaning forward out of the window, Reilly dry-retched then spat. The cold air on his sweaty brow sent a shiver through him.

"But we found the stolen car five hundred yards up the road. Sir?"

Breathless and unsteady on his feet, Reilly sank back to perch on the edge of the bath and rested his forehead in his hands, taking deep breaths to calm his rapid heart rate.

"He was here," said Reilly.

A warm hand found his shoulder, and Cole knelt in front of him.

"Sir?" she said, her voice a whisper in the spinning room. "I'll take care of this. You need to go."

"No," replied Reilly, aware of his slurred words. He swallowed hard, forced his eyes wide to focus and found Mills staring back at him from where she was kneeling on the floor.

"Sir, leave this to me," said Cole, squeezing his shoulder. "I'll get her processed and you can meet me at headquarters. Go see a doctor."

"You," said Reilly, pointing his shaking finger at Mills. "Where is he?"

Mills said nothing.

"Sir, let me get her processed. I can take care of it," said Cole, as Reilly stood from his perch and staggered a little, but used the wall to step past Mills into the hallway.

"What's his name?"

"Sir, let me take care of it," said Cole.

"She isn't going to headquarters," said Reilly, finding a clarity of vision in his anger. He bent his knees to crouch in front of Mills. "She's going underground and she's going to tell us everything she knows."

"Sir, she's one of us," said Cole.

"So she should know what to expect," replied Reilly, easing himself to full height. "Get her hooded and get her to the facility."

CHAPTER THIRTY

"First we thread the hose through here," said Lucas, as he fed the orange gas line through a series of small loops in a bag he had modified. "Then we pull it tight."

He tugged on the line and began to crimp a brass gas fitting to the end of the hose.

"Do you see this, Herman? You may have all the computer skills, but when it comes to delivering a slow and painful death..." He looked up at the computer screen on the far side of the room. "I learned from the best."

He gave the fitting one final squeeze with the crimping tool and set it down on his workbench.

"You don't have to do this, Lucas," said Herman. His eyes flicked to the bedroom door, enough for Lucas to notice. "We don't have to kill them."

"Dear brother, you're so weak. So innocent. There's so much you need to learn about life."

"I learned forgiveness," said Herman.

"And I learned revenge," replied Lucas, his tone sharp and cruel. "Forgiveness is for the weak. Forgiveness will weigh on you like a lead weight for as long as you walk the earth, dear brother. No. Revenge will raise your head up high. Revenge will see you standing tall and proud. That's what we need. That despicable wretch of a woman in there, no sooner than when you were out of the picture, she was hoisting up her skirt for all and sundry."

"But my son..." said Herman.

"Your son?" said Lucas. "Your son? Do you honestly think that, right now, that boy sees you as the man he calls his father?"

"But he doesn't know me," said Herman. "Not the real me."

"No. All he knows is that his father is a weak-minded fool who couldn't keep his hands to himself. All he knows, right now, is that his life on this earth was destined to end before it began because of you, his father. Oh no, Herman. When the last breath of air touches that boy's lips, he'll see how strong his father is. He'll wish he knew you. He'll wish his bitch of a mother hadn't opened her legs so readily."

"But we can let him go," said Herman. "The boy deserves a chance. He's seen nothing of the world. He wouldn't tell. I could look after him."

"You can barely look after yourself, dear brother. Look at you. You're wetter than a limp lettuce leaf," said Lucas. "No. We're going to create you a new beginning, Herman. A new life. Look at what you've achieved so far. Look at the list and how far you've come. Forget about the past. Look to the future, dear brother. Think of how bright and glorious the world will be when everybody who ever wronged you is gone, and there only exists freedom. New people with no memory of who you were. New people who will only see a strong man. A confident man. A man that any son would be proud of."

"It seems so far away," said Herman.

"Oh, it's close, Herman. So close you can touch it. There's three more names on that list and soon there'll be none."

Herman tapped the valve of a gas cylinder with the wrench he was holding. He checked the pressure gauge as he turned the black, plastic knob and watched with glee as the hose he'd fixed around the room straightened under the pressure of his home-made concoction.

"Are you sure they'll come?" said Herman, touching the nozzle at the end of the hose as if he might somehow make a connection with the instrument that would bring a close to the chapter in his life.

"Oh, they'll come alright," said Lucas. "One by one, they'll come, and when they do, we'll be ready. Their twitching bodies will be the final scene, a sight you'll recollect for years to come. The sound of them choking will be the symphony that carries you through life. A reminder of your strength. A reminder of how wonderful you are. And a reminder that the poor, sick boy with wandering hands and an appetite for the taboo is long gone. In his place stands Herman Hoffman."

"I wish it was all over," said Herman. "I can't stand the waiting."

"But it's the waiting that's important," said Lucas. "It's the patience, the planning and execution that will bring you success. You remember those words, don't you?"

"I remember," said Herman, hanging his head and finding distraction in the grain of the wooden floor.

"You remember what he did to you, don't you?"

"Of course," said Herman. "How could I forget?"

"Don't you want to see him suffer in the same way? Don't you want him to cry out for forgiveness?"

"Yes," said Herman, his breathing heavy with the thought and guilty pleasure of revenge.

"But what do we think about forgiveness, dear brother?"

"It is for the weak," said Herman.

"And?"

"Forgiveness will weigh me down for all my years to come," said Herman, reciting the words his brother had committed to his memory.

"So what do we do about it?" asked Lucas. "What do we seek in place of forgiveness?"

"Revenge," said Herman. "We seek revenge."

"And why do we seek revenge?"

"Because revenge will raise our heads up high."

"And?" said Lucas, prompting his little brother to continue on his path.

"Revenge will see us standing tall and proud."

"Very good, dear brother," said Herman. "You're so close now. Can you feel it? Can you feel the strength growing inside your body?"

"Yes," said Herman, watching his hands clench and fingers unfurl with fascination.

"It's electrifying, isn't it?" said Lucas, as he pulled his rucksack onto his back and lifted his hood up to cover his face. He took a deep breath, letting the intense power surge through him, tensing his muscles and breathing hard to push the feeling through his body, prolonging the sensation.

He slammed the flat of his foot against the bedroom door, sending it crashing back into the wall behind. The boy cowered at the noise, still blinded by the hood. Martina tensed, preparing to defend herself.

Lucas watched, marvelling at the effect such a simple action can have on the human psyche. He waited for Martina to stop struggling against her restraints then stepped into the room and, with a deft whip of his hand, he removed the boy's hood.

"It's time," said Lucas.

CHAPTER THIRTY-ONE

The flashing blue lights of a single police car danced off the houses at the end of the street. Two uniformed policemen stopped each car as it entered or left the street to question the driver and passengers, while another managed the traffic, stopping them and waving them on when the questioning was over.

Overhead, a helicopter patrolled, shining its bright spotlight along the maze of alleyways and back streets.

Harvey stood in the shadows contemplating his next move, one hundred yards away from the roadblock.

The voice played over and over in Harvey's mind. The spiteful words were spoken with the same timid and monotone voice that accompanied the pale eyes from the restaurant. Familiarity teased at Harvey's memory. But the thought was broken as a car cruised past the alleyway where Harvey waited.

At the end of the alleyway, parked on the side of the road, were four cars. Each of them were large four-door saloons and no more than a year old. Checking both ways, Harvey stepped out onto the road and crouched beside the first car. To his right, about seven hundred yards away, the house raid was clear in the dark night with a riot of spinning blue lights and activity.

The roadblock had been called in almost immediately.

Whoever was in charge was a seasoned policeman and would be hot on Harvey's tail.

He pulled his knife from the sheath on his belt and lay on the cold, tarmac road. The space was tight, but he shuffled underneath the car, fumbling until his fingers found the fuel line. He slid out of the gap and waited for the trail of fuel to reach the roadside and trickle to a safe distance. Then, with a cursory glance left and right to check the police hadn't closed in, he produced the lighter from the stolen car.

A car was being checked by the roadblock police. One of the men was searching in the back of the car, while the other questioned the single occupant who answered in a loud, irritated tone that carried into the night.

The car was released and the driver put his foot down in a weak attempt to demonstrate his frustration at being stopped in his own street. The noise provided cover for Harvey to strike the lighter. But just as he did, the helicopter roared past overhead, banked, and then returned.

In an instant, Harvey dropped to the ground and shuffled under the car once more. The space was heavy with the smell of fuel and he could feel the petrol soak through his already damp clothes. The helicopter seemed to hover for a moment, its searchlight brushing by the ground where he'd been standing a few seconds before. Then it moved off to search the alleyway from where he'd come.

The alley was long and straight. Harvey had run its length in under two minutes and gauged how long the helicopter search party would be occupied for. Sliding out onto the path, Harvey rolled in a patch of grass to remove any surplus fuel from his jacket. Then, with his heart pumping like a steam train, he checked left and right and lit the fuel, stepping back the instant the fumes caught the flame.

The trail of fuel took light with immediate effect and, with a loud rush and whoop, popped into life beneath the car. A single police officer came running from the roadblock, talking into the radio that was fixed to his shoulder. He was joined by the other two uniforms. They spread out to stop any traffic from passing and maintained a safe distance in case the petrol tank ignited and blew.

The distraction allowed Harvey to slip past the unmanned road-block, out of the side street, across the main road and into Wimbledon Common to lose himself in the mass of trees. He tore a new path in the long grass, stumbling on clumps of vegetation but pushing on, running with everything he had. His heart raced but found rhythm in his steps. His ears, tuned into the sound of the heli-copter, were on high alert, and his eyes, accustomed to the dark, sought new ways out.

It was ten minutes later when Harvey stopped beneath a tree on Wimbledon Common with the road far behind him and a vast pocket of dark forest and footpaths before him. He paused for breath, leaning against the trunk and running the words over and over in his mind.

"Find the place where long grass grows, between three trees and then you'll know."

Sliding his back down the tree to a crouch, Harvey closed his eyes and listened to the voice in his head. The monotone taunts. The childish humour.

Those eyes.

He pictured the eyes in the darkness, pushing the voice from his head, quietening his mind until the eyes, only the eyes, existed.

The trees.

The shadows.

The eyes.

No monotone voice.

Harvey stood.

The eyes peered at him from the forest. Clear and pale. As if they called to him.

He ran into the forest, blind to his surroundings, following only the pale gaze that taunted him.

A memory.

He had it.

It was so close.

He glanced left then right, searching for the memory, the recollection.

A break in the trees up ahead.

The place.

Three hundred yards away.

It was a spot he could never forget.

Trees reached down to whip at his face and low bushes linked arms across the path, nearly bringing Harvey down as he stumbled through the trees in the pitch black. But nothing would stop him.

He burst into a clearing. Three trees in a triangle framed the spot, blocking the wind and allowing only the moonlight to touch the grass that covered the place he'd been before during the same cold, winter moon.

Harvey dropped to his knees, memories of a struggle running riot in his mind. He pulled at the clumps of grass, tossing them to one side and leaving a patch of bare earth. He jammed a broken tree branch into the dirt, scouring deep lines in the soil until it was loose enough to dig with his hands then scoop out.

Then, when the loose soil was removed and the ground became too hard, he started again.

Scour. Dig. Scoop. Scour. Dig. Scoop.

He was an arm's length deep when his fingers found the rocks he'd placed inside the hole so many years before. He raised one, pulling it free of the earth and dragging it through the dirt. He reached into the hole, expecting to find those memories, cold, hard and dead.

But he found nothing lying beneath.

Fingers searched the dirt, waiting for the sickening touch of decay. He pushed himself, tearing out the rocks with both hands and tossing them to one side.

But he found nothing.

He pulled more dirt out.

Scour. Dig. Scoop. Widening the grave with frantic jabs of the stick.

But still, beneath the disturbed rocks lay nothing but cold soil and a space where ancient memories had once been.

Dejected, Harvey fell back onto the grass behind, drawing his knees up to his chest and hugging them close with his filthy arms.

Somewhere, far away in the sky, the helicopter banked, widening its search.

But Harvey stared into the hole, reliving the night. The wait in the darkness. The struggle. The guilty cries of the man. But no name came to him.

The muffled screams and begging. Tears that cut through blood.

But no name came to him.

The wild eyes that begged for mercy as the first shovelful of soil covered his wretched body.

No name found the memory.

The smell of the condemned accepting death with one foot in the next life.

Still no name came to him.

And when all that remained was a hose pipe in the ground to feed the man air.

He stared up at the moon, sucked in a lungful of air and whispered as those pale eyes took form. White skin, as if it had never seen the light of day, emerged and surrounded the eyes, and a breath of thin, blonde hair, parted neither this way nor that, or styled in any way, shape or form, hung across his forehead.

The look of fear took hold as Harvey's memory played the scene over and over. His eyes widening. His mouth parting to scream.

Like a sting to Harvey's heart, the name found his lips.

"Herman Hoffman."

CHAPTER THIRTY-TWO

Cold, concrete walls, still damp from the recent hosing down, offered a bleak setting, perfect for breaking the minds of those who opposed the nation. Closing the steel door behind him, Reilly began to pace the circumference of the room, letting the heels of his shoes click on the bare concrete floor.

In the centre of the rear wall, a second door led to the unknown, a place where Reilly had only seen people go, often never to return.

At the table in the centre of the room, Mills sat with her hands cuffed behind her back and a hood pulled down tight over her head.

The hosing down had done little to improve the smell that lingered from years of countless beatings, torture and destruction of souls from the team who ran the operation.

"You're familiar with the process, I assume?" said Reilly.

As ever, Mills said nothing.

"It's just you and me right now, but when I give the word, we'll be joined by others," said Reilly, searching for a twitch, a movement of any kind. But he found none. "You'll know from experience that this place doesn't exist. The men that run the facility, they don't exist either. It's a place of forgetting, kind of like an oubliette. Do you know what an oubliette is, Miss Mills?"

No response.

"Let me enlighten you. Oubliette is a French word. It means a place to forget. The French would build dungeons that were only accessible from a small hole many metres above the space. Once they dropped the prisoner inside, there was no escape. Death would come slowly to the prisoner who would wither and die. Of course, we're not going to drop you into a hole. We're not going to give you time to starve. But you will be forgotten. Nobody knows this place exists. Nobody knows you are here. Nobody can hear you scream."

Reilly stopped his pacing and turned to face Mills, allowing a pause, long enough for her to digest his words.

"Unless, of course, you talk," said Reilly. "I want to explain my perspective. Just so we are clear here and there are no misunderstandings."

He began his pacing again, circling the table while he thought about the best place to begin the story.

"Three days ago," he began, "a gas bomb was detonated in Jubilee Gardens. Many innocent people died on the scene. Many more died a slow, painful death from their injuries."

He stopped opposite Mills and rested his hands on the chair in front of him.

"Have you ever seen a man choke to death on his own blood? Have you ever seen a child suffocating on their own swollen lungs and throat?" asked Reilly. "It's not a pretty sight. The very next day, an identical gas bomb was detonated in Victoria Embankment Park. It was a callous and vicious attack on defenceless people who stood no chance at all. More deaths. More innocent lives lost. But we got a break, a real chance at catching the bomber."

The pacing began once more as Reilly thought back to the footage they'd watched on Cole's tablet.

"Just seconds before the second bomb detonated, we found two people running into the park. A man and a woman. The woman, if you haven't guessed, is yourself, Miss Mills, and she had her face covered by a scarf. The man, who appears not to exist in any records anywhere in the country, is holding a phone and he's making a call."

Her body tensed as he rested his hands on her shoulders. Then she shrugged him off. But Reilly held her in place, his grip tightening.

"So, you see how this looks, Miss Mills," said Reilly, "when we find the homemade device with a detonator rigged to be triggered by a phone call? Is there anything you'd like to say at this point, Miss Mills?"

But Mills remained silent.

Snatching the hood from her head, Reilly watched as Mills' eyes adjusted to the single bright light and searched the room.

"I told you we're alone," said Reilly. "And I told you this is your chance to talk. After this, I can't help you. The men here know far more ways to extract information than I do, and with less accountability. You can imagine how efficient they are."

Mills stared back at him across the table with an almost blank gaze, unfazed by the facility's less than welcoming charm.

"Imagine how intrigued we were when we saw you both run to the train station," said Reilly, keen to progress his side of the story and to start developing hers. "But wait. Two of you entered the train station. And we have a witness who has made a statement that he saw you both in what appeared to be a tense conversation as the train was brought to a stop. He goes on to say that both of you got off the train with the other passengers. But only one of you emerged onto the platform."

As expected, Mills offered no insight. Instead, she held his gaze, waiting for him to continue.

"I'll tell you where he went," said Reilly. "He walked back to Embankment, tied up a member of staff, and killed the lights in the station before escaping in a taxi, which he then switched somewhere near Elephant and Castle. From there, we lost him. He's a very resourceful man, Mills. But not as resourceful as me."

The comment failed to raise an emotion from Mills, who remained unsurprised and unimpressed.

"Then, earlier today, yet another bomb detonates. A restaurant in Fulham. And who do we find running from the scene? Your friend, Miss Mills. And, as if that wasn't bad enough, we chased him and he ran. A guilty man running for his life, prepared to face death in the River Thames rather than face the consequences of his own actions."

Mills' eyes closed, as if she was hearing the story for the first time and couldn't bear to imagine the man she was protecting jumping to his death.

"But he didn't die, did he? He'd have us believe he was dead. But no. He's not as smart as he thinks he is. He came to see you. He came to see you, didn't he? Because you're the only thing he has in his life. Am I right, Miss Mills? We know he came to see you. We know he stole a car to get there because we found it. And we know he escaped because the fire brigade are putting out the fire he started as we speak. He's cunning, Mills. But not as cunning as me."

Reilly let his last words hang in the air, tempting Mills to speak. Anything. The first words were often the opening of floodgates. A monosyllable. A murmur or a whisper. It didn't matter. All he needed was a single sound and he knew he would have her.

The silence was broken by the slamming of a steel door along the long corridor outside.

"You're running out of time," said Reilly. "They're coming and there's absolutely nothing I can do to stop them when they arrive."

Mills remained silent.

"Mills, talk to me. You're one of us. Don't do this. Help me stop him."

Her eyes softened.

"Mills, you know what happens here. I don't need to lie to you. If these men take you, the chances of you getting out alive are slim. They receive their instructions from much higher up the food chain than me. Help me find him. Tell me his name at least. Give me something to go on."

A knock at the door added urgency to Reilly's tone.

"Mills, look at me," said Reilly, meeting her distant stare. "They'll make you disappear and when they find your friend, they'll tear him to bits."

But still, Mills said nothing.

Slamming his hand on the steel-plated desk, Reilly felt his heart rate jump into action, thudding against his chest, and felt his course breathing shallow. It was coming. He knew it was coming.

Another bang on the door.

"Sir, it's time," said a man's voice from outside.

"If you can't do it for me, Mills, do it for the people out there. The innocent people."

Another bang on the door.

Reilly stood, panting for breath. He plunged his shaking hand into his pocket and felt for the bottle of pills.

Mills stared up at him, defiance in her eyes.

"Sir, open the door," said the man in the corridor outside.

"I can't help you anymore," said Reilly softly, and reached for the door handle.

Two guards walked either side of him, strode to Mills' side and tilted the chair back. The second man opened the door at the back of the room for the other to pull Mills into the dark space beyond. He tracked her eyes as they darted from man to man and searched the new space around her.

But just as the door began to shut and Reilly's eyes closed with the failure and potential consequences, a strong female voice called out.

"Harvey Stone."

The men stopped and turned back to Reilly for a decision, whose mind processed the words with individual scrutiny. The name. The slither of hope that appeared like a light in a dark tunnel. His eyes opened and he turned back to face her.

"His name is Harvey Stone," said Mills. "Untie me and I'll help you find him."

CHAPTER THIRTY-THREE

"There's something you need to know," said Mills. "Remove the cuffs and I'll talk. We don't have long."

Gauging her sincerity with practiced eyes, Reilly nodded at the two men in black who removed the cuffs.

"You get one chance," said Reilly. "Mess up and you'll be dragged back there and never seen again."

"I know how it works," said Mills.

"Then you'll know I'm not lying," said Reilly.

"The goons stay out," said Mills, gesturing at the two men.

Reilly waved them forwards and closed the door behind them, leaving him and Mills alone in the room. Then he leaned into the corridor.

"In here, Cole," he called, and listened as Cole's heels clicked along the hallway.

He closed the door when she arrived. Reilly took a seat beside Cole and opposite Mills, and laid his hands flat on the desk.

"What I have to tell you is top secret. It goes against the official secrets act and about a hundred non-disclosures," said Mills.

Out of the corner of his eye, Reilly caught Cole's reaction, glancing at him and then back at Mills.

"The room is not bugged. The room does not exist. The facility does not exist. Any conversations did not happen," said Reilly.

"Good," said Mills. "You know who I am?"

"Melody Mills," said Cole, opening her file. "Fifteen years across various police services with an exemplary record, including several years working with organised crime, undercover work and several years unassigned."

Mills nodded. "Do you know what unassigned means?"

"It usually indicates that you were assigned to something the agency would prefer not to be accountable for," said Reilly.

"Exactly," said Mills. "It was SO-10."

"And I'm guessing Stone was part of it too? He was also SO-10?"

"How far does your clearance go?" asked Mills, directing the question at Reilly.

"Far enough that I rarely need to ask for permission."

"You're going to need it for this."

"You want me to do some research?" asked Reilly.

"Harvey Stone doesn't exist," said Melody. "He's one of the best operatives SO-10 ever had, but he doesn't exist. He's put his life on the line for this city more times than you can imagine, but he doesn't exist."

"Why is that?" asked Cole. "SO-10 had dozens of operatives. I can pull their files without any clearance at all."

"But they aren't Harvey Stone," said Mills.

"What makes Stone different?" asked Reilly.

"You'll know when you meet him."

"I asked you what makes Stone different, Mills. I told you. You get one chance before that door opens and you cease to exist."

"He's a killer," said Mills, taking a long, slow breath and releasing it through flared nostrils. "I wish I could fluff it up for you, but it's a fact. He was raised by a crime family, trained by a contract killer and has been killing since he was a teenager."

"And you're protecting him?" said Cole. "I don't see how a man like that would be employed by a government agency, officially or unofficially. In fact, he sounds like the type of man that wouldn't lose sleep over a few gas bombs."

"Let's just say his morals are in the right place," said Mills.

"Who did he kill?" asked Cole.

"Bad people," said Mills. "Sex offenders. Rapists. Child molesters. Plus whoever the family needed him to."

"He was a vigilante?" said Cole.

"He had issues," said Mills. "It was his way of dealing with them."

"I'm pretty sure SO-10 don't accept transfer requests from murderers, Mills," said Reilly. "Even if they are cleansing the city. This has all the hallmarks of a plan to buy him time. I don't need to remind you of the position you're in, Mills."

"He was exonerated in return for his services to the City of London. He spent three years saving this city with the threat of prison hanging over him every second of every day."

"So what do we need clearance for?"

"We're going to need access to Harvey's file."

"You just told us he doesn't exist," said Cole. "And now there's a file on him?"

"Harvey Stone exists on paper in one place and one place only," said Mills.

"The director of British Special Forces," said Reilly, falling in with where Mills was going. "That would be the highest level of classification inside any special operations."

Mills nodded.

"And you expect me to call the director of British Special Operations and ask him for a file on a man that doesn't exist? You understand how long that might take?"

"He's the prime suspect in a national terrorism threat," said Mills. "I'm sure the matter can be expedited."

"Right now, we have every police officer in London hunting for him."

"Right now," said Mills, raising her voice for the first time, "you have every police officer in London hunting for the only man who can save thousands of lives."

"And what makes you think Stone's file is going to help?" asked Cole.

"Because that file contains the names of every person he killed."

"A list of dead people?" said Cole.

"And how is that going to help us?" asked Reilly.

"Because one of those dead people is the gas bomber. You're going after the wrong guy."

CHAPTER THIRTY-FOUR

In the distance, the helicopter had widened its search area. Police cars patrolled the main roads like wild animals on the prowl. Harvey stood in the shadows of the forest while the city prepared for the biggest party of the year.

Groups of people walked along the footpaths in the common. Families walked to see the New Year's fireworks. Teenagers stalked in packs, clutching bottles of cheap alcohol and looking for a park bench or a quiet place to celebrate. Couples walked hand in hand, a civilised bottle of wine in a bag, maybe heading to a friend's house for a dinner party.

But for Harvey, there would be no celebrations. With every police officer in London looking for him, and just the name of a dead man to hunt, there was only one place to begin.

He fell in behind a small group who walked beside the road. It was two couples, each walking hand in hand with their partners, reminiscing about the previous years' celebrations. Traffic had started to build on the main road so, with his hands in his pockets to hide the dirt, Harvey kept pace with the foursome until they crossed the road, stepping between the stationary cars to the other side.

Harvey watched them cross. He considered following them but it was too late. The move would look false and create attention. So he continued straight, aware of the heads turning in the endless line of cars that sat in the evening traffic.

A cold wind whipped at Harvey's jacket and stung his ears. But with each passing step, the vision became clearer and the physical discomfort eased, replaced by hope, leaving only unanswered questions and the unknown to fog his mind.

With his head down low and his hands in his pockets, he passed the slow moving cars, only for them to catch him when the traffic lights turned green. A few minutes later, the same cars passed and Harvey felt the same stares.

A police helicopter flying into the wind caught him by surprise when it appeared above the rooftops of the houses on the far side of the road. The thundering noise of the rotors was sudden and its huge spotlight lit the street with inescapable scrutiny. Harvey glanced up once, watched it pass, but maintained audible contact to gauge its distance as it ran its spotlight in long sweeping arcs across the common. Harvey continued his walk, retracing the journey and racking his mind for details his brain had long since tucked away somewhere cold and dark.

Flashes of newspapers that Harvey had read while researching the kill.

Those eyes.

An image of a brick building buried in the shadows of a dark alleyway. A sliding steel door with two huge, round garbage bins outside. And a smell. He remembered a smell. It hadn't been thick or putrid, just evident, as if it the air was permanently stained or ingrained in the structure of the building. It had clung to the back of his throat.

A row of trees had lined the perimeter fence as if somehow adding some green would counter the industrial look of the place.

The faces of dozens of Harvey's victims rolled through his memory as if they were on a carousel. He saw not the pained expressions moments before their last breaths like the faces that haunted his dreams, but the shocked and fearful faces they'd worn when they realised their dirty games were up and the remaining moments of their life would be unbearable.

Audible gasps of guilt.

Mouths hung open in disbelief and fear.

Postures slumped in self-loathing and cowardice.

And eyes widened when they saw the cold, hard stare that Harvey offered them.

Those eyes.

A car horn beeped in unison with screeching tyres, shaking Harvey from his trance-like state, and the images he'd recalled faded once more. He stopped in the middle of the road his subconscious had steered him to cross.

A man rolled down his car window and leaned out.

"Hey," he called, shrugging off his wife's attempts to stop him. "You want to watch where you're going, mate. I could have killed you."

Slowly, Harvey turned to face him, aware of the approaching helicopter and fighting the urge to retaliate. But the man hadn't finished. Harvey stared back at him, clinging to the memory of the brick building, the trees and the smell.

"Get out of the road," shouted the man, as two more cars pulled up behind him and began to honk their horns.

Harvey didn't reply.

It was coming. The memory. The pieces were there. The route he'd taken when he'd followed Hoffman that night. It was the junction where he stood.

When he'd dragged Hoffman into the common.

The road opposite where he stood seemed so familiar, differing only in age. The common to Harvey's left and behind, and the houses to his right. The journey Harvey had taken, keeping to the shadows as Hoffman had navigated the maze of back streets, played in reverse.

Another car joined in the chorus of horns, all aimed at Harvey, urging him to get out of the road.

"Right, mate," said the man in the lead car, as he pushed open his car door. "It's your bleeding funeral."

He slammed his door on his wife's hysterical objections and walked towards Harvey as more car drivers joined in vocalising their outrage via their horns. He ran his hand across his balding head and rolled the cuffs up his thick arms as he approached.

"You've got three seconds to move out of the way, mate," said the balding man, as he drew closer to Harvey. "One," he said from a few feet away.

Harvey didn't reply. He stared at the road ahead, piecing the puzzle together.

"Two," said the man. A tiny piece of spittle flew from his mouth, his emotions firing on all cylinders.

Harvey turned his head to look at the man, whose rage was distracting him from the memories.

"Funeral?" said Harvey, as a connection was made and the journey in his mind was complete.

"Three," said the man with finality, and drew his arm back to swing a punch at Harvey.

The memory was complete. The fragments of memories came together in a moment of clarity. With lightning-fast reflexes, Harvey's hand shot up and took hold of the bigger man's throat mid-swing. The punch faltered and, as predicted, the man's arm shot to Harvey's hand to release his iron grip.

"You're a genius," said Harvey, then ran across the road and disappeared into the now familiar side street.

CHAPTER THIRTY-FIVE

"We need the names of every person killed or injured in all three attacks," said Mills. She fingered the plastic label on the front of the binder as if she was recalling a memory.

"We don't have time to find a link, Mills," said Reilly. "Are you going to open that or what? You do realise I've committed to this now, don't you? The director will be wanting results and so far all we have is your name and the name of a guy that doesn't exist."

"Actually, sir, the PM wants an update in thirty minutes," said Cole. "The city is on high alert and it's too late to stop the celebrations. It would cause mayhem and panic, which could potentially be as bad as another attack."

"So you see, Mills," said Reilly, "Harvey Stone is all we have. So if you can't piece this together, I'll have no choice but to bring him in."

She stared back at him, still clutching the binder to her chest.

"It won't come to that," she said. Then, as if a switch had been flipped, the emotion disappeared from her face and she slammed the folder onto the desk. "Where's that list of victims?"

Seeking approval, Cole glanced at Reilly, who gave her the nod. Two blue paper folders as thick as a phone book were pulled from

Cole's bag and she took the seat opposite Mills. It was as if the fact that Mills was the only suspect in custody had been forgotten and she was now on the team.

"Just remember," said Reilly, "you're still a suspect in a terrorist attack. You're still in the facility and nobody knows you're here."

"I remember," replied Mills, keeping her head down as she flicked through the pages of Stone's file. "I should remind you that we have six and a half hours until the clock strikes twelve. So you can either stand there making idle threats or you can get in here and help us."

Both Cole and Reilly glanced at each other then back at Mills, who felt their stares and looked up at them, flicking from one to the other with her eyebrows raised in question.

"What?" she said.

"What happens when the clock strikes twelve?" said Reilly. "Is there something we should know?"

Keeping her place in the binder with the flat of her hand, Mills let the pages fall closed and sucked in a deep breath.

"The fireworks," she said.

"What about them?" asked Reilly.

"Well, if you were a terrorist planning an attack on New Year's Eve, when would you detonate your bomb?"

"But I'm not a terrorist," said Reilly.

"Well, you need to learn to think like one," said Mills, opening the binder again. "If we're going to catch this guy, you need to be him. You need to live him. You need to breathe him. Right now, he's two steps ahead of us and there's a million people out there who need us to work together. Are you in? Or are you going to continue to disrupt us?"

Reilly digested the outburst. He scratched his chin and stared at the woman who seemed so confident.

"And if you can't stop that hand shaking, just have a drink. It's in your pocket," said Mills.

Cole slowly turned her head to offer Reilly a knowing look. He opened his mouth to speak.

"I can smell it on your breath," said Mills.

"It's medicinal," said Reilly, as he took the seat next to Cole, reddening with both anger and embarrassment.

Flicking through the binder with one hand and making notes with the other, Mills seemed too distracted to hear him. Reilly pulled the second thick, blue binder across the desk and busied himself by flicking past the introductory pages of the report to the details of each victim.

"There's not many ailments out there that can be treated with scotch," said Mills without looking up.

Reilly stopped, aware that Cole hadn't offered him her look again.

"Some things just aren't treatable with medicine," said Reilly. "Some things require a little help just to get through the day."

"Well, how about you find me a connection to one of these guys," said Mills, spinning the sheet of paper on the desk for them both to read.

"Who are these?" asked Cole, looking up from her list of names.

But Mills didn't reply. Her look said it all.

"These are Stone's victims? How did you shortlist the names?" asked Reilly. "It could be any one of those people in that file."

"Correction," said Mills. "It can't be any of them. They're dead."

"So how did you come up with the list?" said Cole.

"You really need me to explain?" said Mills, flicking her eyes between the two of them. She sighed then opened the binder and spun around to face them, moving her list to one side. A polished and manicured nail rested on the name of Stone's first victim, while her other hand held the wad of papers bent and ready to flick through. "This guy was found with his limbs burned off. This guy was found boiled in a bathtub. This guy was found hanging from a crane."

She continued to flick through each sheet, identifying the manner of death and the state of the bodies as they were found.

"And this guy was discovered glued to a bathtub with his entrails in his lap and his testicles in his mouth," finished Mills.

She closed the binder and turned it back towards her to avoid the obscene photos being on show.

"And the list?" said Reilly, covering for Cole, who had fallen silent at the sight of the images and the descriptions Mills had provided.

"That's easy," said Mills. "Their bodies were never found."

The silence was broken by Cole's phone vibrating on the desk. Reilly fixed Mills with a stare then nodded for Cole to answer the call. She stood from the table and stepped into the corridor, but returned before the door had time to close.

"Sir," she said, glancing at Mills then back at Reilly, "Harvey Stone has been spotted in Wimbledon. He attacked a member of the public. All units are on stand-by."

Mills' face dropped like a stone in the sea and her head fell forward in defeat.

Reilly opened his mouth to talk but nausea got the better of him. He swallowed hard, feeling his throat close and his chest tighten.

"Sir?" said Cole. "What do you want us to do?"

He opened his mouth to breath, but found nothing but sharp stabs in his lungs and a pounding heart.

"Sir?" said Cole.

"What's happening?" said Mills, as the sensation eased and Reilly's airways opened up. A burning red covered the skin on his face and a layer of cool sweat formed on his brow.

"Sir, are you okay?" said Cole. "You need to see someone."

"Just go," said Reilly, catching his breath and clearing his throat of phlegm.

"I can't leave you like this," said Cole.

"You'll do as you're damn well told and that's an order," said Reilly, leaning on the table to steady himself. "And you can take her with you. She might be useful. I'll be fine. I'll be right behind you."

CHAPTER THIRTY-SIX

"Are we going to watch the fireworks?" asked the boy, holding the hands of his mum and Herman as they made their way through the crowds of people in London's Parliament Square. He looked up at his mum then across to Herman, who smiled back at him.

"Quiet, Sam," said Martina, offering Herman a warning look.

"Of course, son," said Herman. "Have you ever seen fireworks?"

"Don't you talk to my son," said Martina. Her face screwed up and her voice lowered to avoid causing a scene. "It's bad enough you brought us here. You're sick."

"I think you're forgetting who's in charge," said Lucas. "Do I need to remind you what's in your little backpacks? One wrong move, Martina, and it's game over for you."

Her hand touched the strap across her chest, where a small black padlock fixed it in place. Herman watched as her eyes fell to the boy's backpack, a smaller version of her own but otherwise matching. The same joyful blue. The yellow beading around the edges. And the same black padlock to stop it from being removed.

"I didn't want to do this," said Herman. "I didn't want-"

"Don't talk to me," said Martina. "Or my son."

"If Herman wants to talk to his son, Martina, you should let him. Every boy needs to hear his father's voice once in a while."

"Stay out of this, Lucas."

"I'll stay out of nothing. Let the boy talk if he wants. Let the boy see what a good man his father really is."

"Herman Hoffman is-"

"Misunderstood, Martina. My dear brother is misunderstood. That's all."

They moved to the side of the road to let a group of people dressed as farmyard animals through, and the boy smiled in delight as the giant pig made a show of scratching his back side and trying to straighten his tail.

"Do you like farmyard animals?" said Herman, crouching to be the same level as the boy.

He nodded.

"Do you have a favourite animal?" asked Herman.

The boy thought for a while, biting his lower lip and glancing up to his mum for approval. She feigned a smile and nodded for him to answer.

"Dogs," said Sam.

"Dogs?" replied Herman, with a little too much enthusiasm. "We had a dog when we were your age. Do you want to know his name?"

Sam nodded, not taking his eyes off Herman.

"His name was Conrad and he was black," said Herman, "with a long, furry tail and big droopy ears."

"Was he a good dog?" asked Sam.

"He was the best," replied Herman, and ruffled Sam's hair.

He stood and stared at Martina.

"He likes me," said Herman.

"He's a child. He doesn't know any better," said Martina.

"Let's go," said Lucas. "We don't have time to chit chat." He found a gap in the crowd and pulled the family along until they all walked side by side, bunched together to avoid being separated.

"Don't try anything stupid, Martina," said Lucas. "My brother may be soft, but I have a much firmer hand."

"Where are we going?" asked Martina.

"To see the fireworks, of course," replied Lucas, flicking his eyes down to the boy and back to meet Martina's hate-filled stare. "It'll be a night to remember."

"You know there'll be a thousand police here? You won't get away with anything."

"I won't be needing to get away with anything, Martina," said Lucas, as he pulled them to the side of the road overlooking the river.

"This seems like a nice spot, doesn't it, Sam? What do you think?" said Herman, and leaned down to pick up his son. The move sparked Martina's fears. She cried out and reached to pull Sam away. But Herman held him tight, moving him out of Martina's reach.

"No. Don't," she said, above the din of the crowd.

"What are you doing?" said Herman, and smoothed Sam's hair. "You do trust me with my own flesh and blood, don't you?"

But Martina just stared at him.

"You trust me, don't you, Sam?" said Herman, the tone of his voice as childish as his son's.

The boy nodded and peered down at the water, marvelling at the reflections of the city lights against the inky, black river.

The crowd flowed past in waves of what seemed like thousands at a time, but the spot they had chosen was out of the flow, like the outside of a meandering river bend.

"Are you my daddy?" asked Sam, with the inquisitive confidence of a child.

The question hit Martina hard. In the corner of Herman's watering eye, he saw her turn away, unable to look, as if he was some kind of monster.

Herman thought on his response. He wanted to cry out 'yes'. He wanted the crowd to know. Instead, he just nodded and let Sam wipe the tear from his eye. They shared a smile, father and son, and for the first time for as long as Herman could remember, there was happiness in his world.

"Daddy," said Sam, eliciting a further grimace from Martina, who stood a few feet away.

"Yes, son?" said Herman, then cleared his throat.

"What happened to Conrad?" asked Sam, his head cocked to one side as Herman's often did.

Herman bit his own lower lip. He swallowed hard and was about to speak when Lucas opened his mouth and stole the moment from him.

"The same thing that happens to all of us, Sam," said Lucas, his tone hard and sharp.

"No," said Herman. "No, don't."

"What's that?" asked Sam.

"He was killed."

CHAPTER THIRTY-SEVEN

The smell hit Harvey first. It was a tangy scent of rot and decay, sweetened by the overbearing chemical smell of disinfectant. He stood in the shadows of the trees that lined the fence, opposite the sliding shutter doors he remembered so well.

He touched the tree, finding the V in the trunk where two branches split that he peered through, exactly as he had done close to ten years before. The lights were off in the building. Dark windows offered no clue of the life inside.

He waited a full minute, enough time to pass for anybody who may have seen him to venture out.

But nobody came.

The steel shutter doors were locked, but the small doorway to the right was open, as if it was inviting Harvey in.

He drew his knife from his belt, checked behind him, and stepped inside.

His footsteps echoed in the darkness and the door slammed shut behind him, killing any ambient light.

A drip of water was the only sound, save for the regular thud of Harvey's heart. He breathed slow and long, controlling his desire to leave. Instead, he edged forward, rolling his boot as he stepped to quieten the noise, until his foot found the first stair and his hand touched the rail.

Step by step, listening to every sound made by the old building, Harvey climbed the concrete stairs, blinded by the darkness but guided by a memory of what once was.

A single doorway, its shape darker than the surrounding wall, stood at the top of the stairs. A round door handle offered itself, its shiny finish contrasting with the dull wood and concrete.

It turned in Harvey's hand and the door opened to reveal more of the smell, the odour of death and bad hygiene, but little to see in the dark space except a flashing green light on the far side of the room.

Harvey stepped inside, his senses tuned for movement and sound. He pulled the door closed behind him, working the handle to avoid the click of the mechanism giving his presence away. The more he searched the darkness, the clearer his vision became as his eyes adjusted to the gloom.

A full minute passed. Shapes became clearer. A single chair in front of a computer desk, which was the source of the flashing green. A window with heavy curtains that blocked any ambient light pulled closed.

Stepping further into the room, Harvey found a bedroom door open. The same heavy curtains blocked the light. A small bed had been placed against the centre of the far wall.

The floorboards creaked under his weight, loud in the silence and amplified by the empty, featureless room.

"Hoffman," said Harvey, and waited for a response.

The flashing green light at the top of the computer screen seemed to beckon him, holding his attention like a hypnotist might distract a patient with a swinging pendant.

But something else caught his eye. At the far end of the room, darker than the shadows that surrounded it, was a shape. The closer Harvey stepped, the clearer the image became, but denial ushered reality away until Harvey's hand touched it, affirming the facts, cold and hard.

Beneath his fingers was the grain of polished wood. He ran his hand from right to left across the surface. Even in the darkness, the craftsmanship was evident. His fingers found the edge of the moulded coffin lid. Every part of him fought to leave it be.

But he had to know.

He had to look.

He lifted the lid and stepped back.

Loving hands had assembled the skeletal remains of the body. Soft, plush material lined the inside of the coffin and was infused with some kind of scent to mask the stale odour of decay.

Harvey dropped the lid, but the image remained as if it had been branded onto his eyes.

Allowing the silence to steady his jumbled flow of thoughts, he stepped back, until the flashing green light once more teased him.

With each flash of the tiny light, Harvey could make out the contents of the small desk. He ran his finger across the pen that lay on top of a large, lined notepad. The lid of the pen was missing and the writing on the pad was neat, far neater even than Melody's methodical and meticulous handwriting.

The light flashed on once more, offering Harvey a short glimpse of the words.

Six names.

Six lines.

Three with hard lines through them as if the culprit had dug the nib of the pen into the paper and dragged through each of the three names with malice and contempt. Harvey ran his finger over the writing, feeling the depth of each line. It was as if each line was deeper than the last.

A growing anger.

But somehow, the angry lines failed to match the timid and weak persona of Hoffman as Harvey remembered him. He was a disturbed man, a victim in the eyes of most who knew him, who found solace and peace working with the dead in the funeral parlour beneath Harvey's feet by day. By night, he would find his prey on Wimbledon common, subjecting his victims to sordid, unthinkable things to mask his own misgivings and weaknesses.

Harvey looked around the room, remembering with new found clarity the images of the children Hoffman had lured there and held captive. While grieving widows arranged the funerals of their loved ones downstairs at the front of the shop, Herman Hoffman would be in the workshop out back, his mind tinkering at the thought of his latest pleasure in the upstairs flat.

Flashes of the newspaper images ran through Harvey's mind, now complete and no longer obscured by the fog of time. The boy in the room that the police had found, starved and hooded. The images on the computer too sick to print. The headline stating that Hoffman had run away and become another man the police would one day stop looking for.

But Hoffman hadn't run away.

Harvey had found him first.

And now the tables were turned.

The green light on the computer stopped flashing, but it stayed lit, casting a green glow across the keyboard. Lowering himself into the chair, Harvey peered at the screen as a window appeared. The word 'connecting' scrolled from right to left at the bottom and a single beep signalled that the connection had been established.

Harvey took a breath, knowing what was to come.

"Harvey Stone," said Hoffman. "I knew you'd find us."

CHAPTER THIRTY-EIGHT

The sound of Cole's heels clicking along the corridor faded to a whisper, then stopped, and the ping of the elevator doors announced their journey up to the ground floor.

Reilly exhaled, loud and deep, emptying his lungs, and spat the blood from his mouth into a tissue. Using the back of a chair to steady himself, he pushed himself to his feet and waited for the head rush to cease.

The smooth corridor wall guided him to a small kitchenette used by the men who ran the facility. Grateful that the room was empty, Reilly fell across the sink, holding onto the draining board with both hands, and let the remaining blood run from his throat. He spat and cleaned the sink then searched for a glass to use to rinse his mouth. Behind him in the centre of the room was a small table with four chairs. A pack of cards, an ashtray and three empty coffee cups had been left for the cleaning contractor.

A small TV had been mounted to the wall to keep the men amused during their breaks and the periods of downtime. The volume was low, barely audible above the noise of the ventilation unit and the thud of Reilly's heart in his ear.

He rinsed his mouth then refilled the glass, certain the attack had passed. Then he turned to lean back on the sink. The ashtray in the centre of the table was overflowing. The remains of the cigarettes seemed so appealing. It couldn't hurt. There was no more damage to be done.

He stepped across to the table, eying the butt with the most cigarette remaining, and picked it up from the piles of ash. Reilly rolled it in his fingers then sniffed in the foul but intoxicating odour.

A small box of Swan Vesta matches had been used as currency for the men's break time card games and several lay sprawled across the table. He placed the glass down and picked up a single match.

He glanced behind him to make sure he was alone and listened for a second for the tell-tale sound of army issue boots on the painted concrete in the corridor.

But he heard nothing.

One strike was all it took for the match to light. He placed the butt in between his lips and raised the flame to the end, raising his head to avoid the heat so close to the two days' growth on his face.

The tobacco crackled like a tiny log fire as the flame grew closer, singeing the end of the butt enough to elicit the foul smell. He gagged as the first tastes of stale tobacco touched the back of his throat and pulled the butt from his mouth, taking deep, painful breaths to hold down the contents of his stomach.

He tried once more.

Raising his face to the ceiling, he lit one more match.

This time he didn't hesitate.

He brought the flame to the butt and inhaled, drawing the heat into the tobacco and feeling the taste as the nicotine found its way to his blood. He closed his eyes and let the smoke crawl from his open mouth, savouring the taste and remembering the days when he'd light a cigarette before even stepping out of bed.

The feeling passed.

He brought the butt up for one last drag, his eyes falling on the TV as he did. A pretty, young news reporter was standing on Westminster Bridge with her hood pulled up and a large microphone held in her gloved hand. Behind her, thousands of people had gathered for the fireworks. A few teenagers vied for a position on camera and waved to their families.

Unable to hear what the reporter was saying, Reilly watched as the camera panned to take in the full view. The thousands turned to millions, a sea of heads as far as the eye could see.

Reilly crushed the cigarette and picked up the glass of water, draining it in one swoop to wash away the foul aftertaste of the tobacco.

The camera continued to pan.

A teenager jumped up from behind a group of people to be seen by the camera. A group of girls waved, giggled then shied, and policemen standing nearby winked at the camera, a proud sign of London's resilience. Even in the midst of a terrorist attack, nothing would stop the city from celebrating as it had done for years.

But standing to one side of the policeman, pressed against the bridge out of harm's way, a family of three caught Reilly's eye. There were no smiles on their faces. The boy looked overwhelmed by the chaos and noise. The mother appeared downtrodden, clinging to her son as if he was everything she had.

And the father.

There was a silence.

A skip of Reilly's heart.

And the glass crashed to the floor.

For a split second, the father's eye met the camera. It was less than a split second, a nanosecond, and then the camera had moved on.

But it had been enough.

Like two iron fists crushed Reilly's chest, another attack came on, squeezing his lungs with a ferocity like never before. He staggered through the door, slipping on the broken glass and pool of water. Then, clinging to the wall, he made his way back to the interview room.

He'd taken three steps before he dizzied and fell to the floor. Clinging to consciousness by a thread, as his head spun with impossibilities, he half-crawled and half-dragged himself to the door.

"Sir?" said a voice behind him. It was a man's voice. A northerner. Reilly recognised his tone as the security guard. He reached up to the number pad to enter the entry code. "Sir, are you okay?" said the guard. From the corner of Reilly's eye, he saw the man begin to run to help him.

"Open the door," said Reilly, with the flat of his hand ready to push it open.

"Sir, should I call someone?" said the guard.

"I said open the damn door," said Reilly. "Please. Just open the door."

Six beeps of various tones signalled the guard entering the code. Then, as Reilly shoved open the door, two strong arms pulled him up and helped him onto one of the chairs.

"What can I do?" said the guard, stepping in front of Reilly.

"Water," said Reilly, breathless and wheezing. "I just need a minute."

The guard shot from the room, radioing for medical assistance while he walked.

The palm of Reilly's hand slapped onto the table, snatching up Stone's file.

Reilly knew it would be in there.

He didn't need to look.

But he did.

Tearing through the pages of the file, flicking past scenes of devastation, torture and sickening human ability until he found what he was looking for.

He gave a moan and closed his eyes as memories began to inch their way into his conscience.

But they called to him. They begged him to look.

From the open page of the file, taunting him with cold malice, framed by white, deathly skin, was a pair of pale, shining eyes.

CHAPTER THIRTY-NINE

The heaving crowd closed in as people found their places to view the annual spectacle, crushing Martina into Herman, who held Sam up high, resting the boy on his hip.

"Please, Martina. Don't look at me like that," said Herman. "I'm different now."

"So stop this," she hissed in reply. "Get us out of here before Lucas comes back."

"I can't," said Herman, checking behind him. "You don't know what he's capable of. If he finds us-"

"Then why?" said Martina, swallowing to restrain the tears that threatened to burst from her. "Why us? Why now?"

With a quick glance at Sam, who was enthralled by his lofty view of the sea of people standing on the bridge, Herman met Martina's eyes then lowered his head.

"You wouldn't understand," said Herman. "You could never understand. Nobody could."

"Help us," said Martina, her eyes pleading with her ex-husband. "We can run away. The three of us. It'll be like old times."

Herman's mouth fell open, picturing the scene. He gently lowered Sam to the ground.

"We could start over, some place new," said Martina, sensing Herman's interest.

"Like a family?" said Herman.

"Yes," said Martina.

"And Sam would have a father?"

"Yes."

"That was what I always wanted."

"Just you, me and Sam, Herman," said Martina. "We can find somewhere remote. Somewhere he'd never find us."

"In the country. I always wanted to live in the country, away from..." Herman's voice trailed away as he cast his eyes across the smiling families, couples and young children waiting with anticipation for the fireworks.

"Away from the people?" asked Martina.

The question roused Herman from thoughts he'd long since buried. He stared at Martina.

"Temptation," he said, his eyes softening. "I'd treat you so well."

"Oh, Herman," said Martina, working her way under his arm. "These past few days, it's been all I could think about, lying there on that bed. Oh, Herman, you would never treat us like that, would you?"

"No," said Herman. "Never. I'd do anything for you. I'd do anything to make it right."

"We have lots of time to make up for, Herman," said Martina, squeezing his hand. "And Sam would love it too. Wouldn't you, Sam?"

The boy didn't flinch at the sound of his name. A pair of circus clowns entertaining the crowd had captured his attention.

"He would," said Martina. "I know he would."

"I could take him for long walks, show him stuff and-"

"And what?" said Martina.

"And be a father to him," said Herman, smoothing Sam's hair. "I want him to be proud of me. He shouldn't have to know about-"

"He doesn't have to know," said Martina. "We'll never speak of it again. It's my fault anyway. I neglected you. I wasn't there."

"Don't speak of it," said Herman. "That was the old me."

"And you can have it," said Martina. "We can have it all, but-"

"But what?" said Herman, his dejection apparent in his tone.

Martina checked around them to make sure nobody could hear, and then leaned in close.

"You have to help us out of these bags," said Martina, raising her lips to Herman's neck.

Feeling her warm breath on his neck, Herman sighed, offering her more of his skin with a lift of his chin.

"Please, Herman. You have the keys in your pocket. Take the bags off before Lucas comes back. We can throw them in the river. Look at all these people."

She nuzzled in closer, finding the spot behind his ear she used to kiss so many years ago.

"Can I hold him?" asked Herman. "I want to feel him. I want him close."

Martina bent and hoisted Sam into the air. She kissed him on the forehead then held Herman's gaze as she passed her son to him.

Like a natural father, Herman leaned to one side so the boy sat on his hip. He turned to Martina but could only smile at the joy and mumble a thank you through the emotion.

"Just unlock the bags, Herman, and we can be free."

But Herman pulled away. "No," he said. "No. We can't."

"But we'll die," said Martina, closing the gap once more. "Come on, Herman. You were always the smarter brother. You were always the one with the brains."

"He's my brother," said Herman. "He's done so much for me. He's made me a man. For the first time, I feel like I'm in control."

"But you are in control, Herman. Don't you see? Look at you. He's trusted you to stand here with us because you're in control. And where is he now? When there's danger? Where is he when there's real work to be done?"

"He's not afraid. He's strong. Stronger than me," said Herman.

"No. Don't ever say that. The Herman I married would never say that. The Herman I married knew the difference between right and wrong," said Martina. "Or maybe that's it? Maybe I was wrong about you? All those years I thought you were dead, and really you were just hiding like the coward you are. All those years I was widowed. I carried Sam for nine months thinking you were dead, hoping and praying you were alive, hoping that the Herman I loved was alive somewhere and that one day you would walk through the door and everything would be alright. But I was wrong, wasn't I? Tell me, Herman. Tell me you're really back. Tell me the Herman I once knew is back and he's going to save us from his evil brother."

The information rolled around Herman's emotional mind. The questions, the statements, the accusations all blended to form some wild concoction that pulled Herman away.

"Where's Lucas?" said Herman. "I need Lucas."

"Unlock us, Herman," said Martina. "Before it's too late."

"I don't know who I am," said Herman. "Lucas saved me. He gave me life. I can't abandon him now. Not when we've come so far."

"Oh, Herman," said Martina, her voice in quiet despair. "He's going to kill us all. Don't you see?"

She gripped him by the arms with enough force to rouse Sam from the excitement around them. Herman pulled away, struggling to find a path between the people around him, trying to get away from Martina, from the incessant questions.

"Herman, listen to me," she said above the noise, and no longer caring for their privacy. "Herman, don't run away."

The crowd shoved him back, defending their positions and the views they'd secured. With his back against the bridge, the angry faces of the neighbouring crowd glared at him and Martina's voice dug deeper into his mind, like ants finding the smallest crevice to get inside. He buried his face into Sam's soft jacket, covering his ear and his eyes with his spare arm.

"No," he said. "No more. Stop."

"Herman, listen to me."

"No. I can't take it."

"Herman, don't do this."

"Leave me alone," he said. His eyes squeezed shut but the wall of sound from all around found its way through any barrier he put up.

"Help us," said Martina.

A surge of emotion rushed from the very pit of Herman's stomach.

He pulled his arm away from his head, raised his head up high and screamed, long and loud. The scream came from inside him. It came from years of pent-up frustration. Of buried secrets. Of hidden truths and lies. Desires that frightened him. Memories that excited him before but sickened him after. And hate. So much hate.

He screamed until all he could hear was his own voice, hoarse, and until the people around him quietened. His eyes squeezed shut, his gut tight from the power the scream pulled from him.

Then he stopped.

He listened to the silence then the murmurs that hummed like a machine.

He opened his eyes to find a space had been made around him. A thousand wondrous eyes. A thousand astonished eyes. A thousand scared eyes.

But as the crowd moved away, huddling closer than before, one man remained where he was with two eyes that bore into him with a malice like no other.

CHAPTER FORTY

"Put the boy down, Hoffman," said Harvey. "There's no way out for you."

He was almost exactly as Harvey remembered him. He had pale skin beyond the paleness of most people. Thin lips framed his imperfect teeth and a small tuft of white blonde hair sat on his chin.

But above all, the feature that identified him more than any other was the pale eyes, unnatural, cold and deathlike.

The woman to Hoffman's side edged away but stayed within reach of her son.

"Stop him," she screamed at Harvey. Her face reddened and the outburst seemed to trigger a burst of tears. She dropped to her knees. "Please, he's got my son."

Harvey took one step closer.

The crowd took a breath.

And Harvey took one more step.

But Hoffman snatched the boy around, holding him over the water.

"I'll do it," said Hoffman. "Get away. One more step and I'll drop him."

The woman to Hoffman's side lunged at him. But Hoffman caught the movement and held the boy further out.

"No, Martina. You can't stop this now. It's gone too far."

The crowd had fallen silent, save for the whispered wonderings of the women, who pulled their own children closer. Phones were pulled from pockets, filming the spectacle like it was some cheap street show.

"Why, Herman?" said Harvey. "Why now? Why these people? It's me you want, not them. Let them go. I'm here."

Harvey raised his arms out to his side to show he was unarmed.

"Take me, Herman. Give the boy back to his mum."

"He's my son," said Herman. "I'm his father. He needs to know his father's a strong man. He needs to see that his father won't be pushed around anymore."

As if on cue, the boy's face crinkled and tears began to roll down his face. He gave off a loud, high-pitched wail and was reaching for his mum, who could do nothing but reach a hand out from where she knelt on the ground, just to let him know she was there. That she was close.

"You want to kill me? Well, here I am," said Harvey. He opened his jacket, raised his shirt and whipped his knife from the sheath on his belt, turning the point to press into his own skin. "You want to see me die? Is that it, Herman? You want to see blood for what I did to you?"

Hoffman's eyes were wide. They flicked from side to side at the crowd then returned to find Harvey.

"Put the boy down, Herman," said Harvey. "And I'll open myself up right here, right now."

The crowd gasped in unison and a small news crew pushed to the front, the camera just three feet from where Harvey stood.

Without warning, Herman brought the boy in from over the water, more from fatigue than his better judgment. His face lost the scared and bitter snarl, dropping into the defeated, downtrodden look that Harvey remembered from the days he spent following him.

The days before his death.

"Do you honestly think this is all about you, Harvey Stone?" said Hoffman, shaking his head and setting the boy on his hip, smoothing his hair to calm him down. "Are you that egotistical that you think everything we've done was to get at you?"

"So why am I here?" said Harvey. "Why are you trying to frame me?"

"You're just a name on a list, Harvey," said Hoffman.

The words were clear.

The meaning was simple.

Harvey could picture the list.

But there was something different about his voice. It carried the same mechanical, monotonous tone, but there was an anger there, a strength that hadn't been there before.

"They all deserved to die, Harvey Stone," said Hoffman, his voice rising as a fury grew behind his pale eyes. "Every man that ever wronged us. The man that touched us as children and warped our fragile little minds. The man that sullied our family, poisoning her with his seed."

Hoffman raised his finger at the woman, who looked up from where she sat crumpled on the ground.

"And you, Harvey Stone," said Hoffman, lowering his hand to his side. "The man that took it all away from us. The man who buried us alive and all our honour along with it."

A murmur from the crowd behind began to grow as people moved further from Harvey.

"That's right," said Hoffman, addressing his audience. "This man here took our lives. Do you remember, Harvey? Do you remember how you forced us to dig a hole with our own bare hands? Do you remember how we pleaded for our life?"

Harvey didn't reply.

"I do," said Hoffman. "I remember you forcing us to lie down in the hole. I remember the first grains of dirt hitting my face as you buried us, with nothing but a hose pipe to breathe through and the weight of the earth crushing our bones."

Harvey stared at him. There was a difference, so subtle he couldn't place it, but it was there in his posture. It was in his voice.

And it was in his eyes.

But the moment was gone.

In an instant, the whole bridge was lit with a bright searchlight, and the deafening roar of rotor blades filled the air as a helicopter rose from beneath the bridge.

The boy's cries were drowned by the thump of the chopper blades, and with renewed vigour, the woman lunged once more. But she was knocked down with one swipe of Hoffman's back hand. He turned to face the helicopter, threatening to drop the boy.

Harvey took a single step forward.

The sea of people moved further away, squeezing together for safety but lingering in sick curiosity.

One man stepped forward from the crowd, parting the way with confident authority. The hum of the crowd quietened once more as the man raised his gun and aimed at Hoffman's back.

Sensing the change in the atmosphere, Hoffman turned his head as if listening for a clue to the disruption. He smiled as the man spoke, whose words cut through the air like a sharp blade through flesh.

"Lucas Hoffman," the man began, stepping further from the crowd to create a triangle between Hoffman, Harvey and himself. "Bring the boy back. Let him go. It's over."

CHAPTER FORTY-ONE

A sharp kick to the back of Stone's legs dropped him to the ground and two strong armed policemen cuffed his hands behind his back.

Reilly glanced at Stone once, studying his face, unable to remove the images of the details in his file.

But Stone's eyes flicked between Reilly and Hoffman as if he was confused.

"Herman," said Stone from his position on his knees. "You don't need to do this."

Hoffman's snarl dropped, softening into a sorrowful look. His posture followed. First his shoulders slumped then his back hunched forward as if the boy's weight was taking its toll.

"You don't understand, Harvey," said Hoffman. "You don't know what he's like. I owe him so much."

"Who, Herman? Who do you owe?" said Stone.

"Lucas," said Reilly. "Lucas Hoffman. You don't fool me. Show yourself."

At the mention of the name, Hoffman's face hardened. His eyes narrowed and his lips thinned to reveal yellowed, uneven teeth.

"It's over, Lucas," said the man. "You remember me, don't you?"

"I remember you alright," said Hoffman. All weakness from his voice had vanished, leaving nothing but cold malice and contempt. "I've waited, oh, so long to see you."

"Well, I'm here now. So put the boy down, Lucas. Enough people have been hurt. Enough people have lost their lives."

"Five long years, Reilly. Five long years we've waited to see you. Planning. Preparation. Patience," said Hoffman, and cast his eyes across to Stone. "Sound familiar, Stone?"

But Stone didn't reply. He knelt on the ground with the armed policemen either side of him, staring back at the deranged, pale-skinned man.

"We've killed them all," said Hoffman. "Every man that ever wronged us."

"We know about your list," said Reilly. "We know about the other men. And we know why we're here."

"They were all for Herman," said Hoffman. "All except you, DCI Reilly. You were for me. You're the last man on our list, and while I sat in that cell, day after day, night after night, I imagined your face as you breathed your last filthy breath."

"That's funny," said Reilly. "You're the last man on my list. But I can't say I ever gave you much thought. You're just another sick individual who should be locked away."

"You can't win them all, Reilly," said Hoffman. "We've thought about this long and hard. Now put the gun down."

A thousand eyes drilled into Reilly's back. He considered giving Hoffman what he wanted, letting the gun falter a little, which raised a smile on Hoffman's face.

But then he straightened and aimed at Hoffman's head, to one side of the boy. He could never take the shot. The risk of hitting the boy was too great. But there was no way he was letting Hoffman get the better of him.

"The boy, Hoffman," called Reilly, as the helicopter's bright searchlight swept across the bridge, the pilot fighting the strong winter winds that rolled off the Thames. "Set him down. He's done nothing to you."

"Don't you understand, Reilly? You all deserve to die," said Hoffman. He pointed his finger at the woman. "She betrayed Herman. She betrayed us both. Couldn't keep her legs together for five minutes, and for that, she dies along with her spawn."

"No," said the woman, who knelt on the ground to Reilly's right, out of Hoffman's vicious reach but close enough for her son to see her. "No, please. Not my son."

"And him," said Hoffman, pointing at Stone. "You know all about him and what he did?"

"He killed your brother," said Reilly.

"And you," said Hoffman. "You locked me up and took away everything we ever had. And for that, for all your sins, you die."

Reilly stepped forward.

The crowd gasped once more.

"Don't come any closer," said Hoffman.

But Reilly took another step.

"Show me Herman," said Reilly.

"No," said Lucas. "He's weak. You'll manipulate him with your cheap tricks."

"Herman," said Reilly, "I want to talk to you."

"No," said Lucas. His face twisted as if fighting some kind of inner battle with his own mind. "No, you can't."

"Herman, your family needs you," said Reilly. "Herman, only you can save them."

The sharp, venomous voice of Lucas faded and the narrowed eyes widened to reveal a scared looking man holding his son. His breathing quickened. His head flicked from side to side as he took in the crowd and their stares. Fear took him in its firm grip.

"I'm dying, Herman," said Reilly. "You can't save me. And Harvey Stone? He's beyond saving. But you can save your family, Herman. You're stronger than he is. Put the boy down, Herman. We're all here. It's just you, me, Stone and her. That's what you wanted, wasn't it?

Well, it's over, Herman. Put the boy down. Nobody needs to get hurt."

With one hand tightly holding the frightened boy, Hoffman backed up against the bridge.

"That's it, Herman," said Reilly. "Just relax. Nobody needs to die here. It's over."

Hoffman's body relaxed once more. He leaned against the balustrade and turned the boy to see his face before lifting him up to kiss his forehead and pull him close.

"You're right about one thing, Reilly," said Hoffman, his face hidden behind the boy. He unzipped the small child's rucksack to reveal the top half of a gas cylinder with a small electrical unit attached to the valve. "This is everything I ever wanted."

He pulled a mobile phone from his jacket pocket and held it high for all to see.

The murmur among the crowd grew to a riot of panicked chatter. Then, as the foremost people identified the contents of the bag and the rumour spread back through them like an ocean wave, the screams started and people began to run.

Children were held high out of harm's way but disappeared from sight as their parents were overcome and trampled. A police horse reared up, kicking out at frantic pedestrians who were forcing a path to safety. It fell to the ground to become another obstacle for the wave of people. One man, seeing no other means of escape, barged past Reilly, knocking the gun from his hands, and hurled himself off the bridge into the river.

Some women screamed somewhere close by, loud and shrill. Reilly turned to find them clutching their children, too scared to run and frozen to the spot as the stampede rushed past in all directions.

As the stampede eased and the bridge emptied of people, groans of pain were all Reilly could hear as he rolled to his side clutching his chest.

A woman screamed for her children who had been swept away

by the crowd. She fell to her knees, unable to decide which direction to search for them.

Only the thundering rotors of the helicopter could be heard as Reilly recovered. A knee had scuffed his face and a boot had stamped on his chest as some poor soul had run for their life.

He lay on his back and took in the sounds.

Gone was the hum of the crowd.

Gone was the chatter of the news reporter.

And gone were the cries of the boy.

He sat up and searched around him to find the bridge empty, save for the injured and the swarm of police running towards him.

The spot where Hoffman had stood was empty, and where Stone had been held, now only a pair of handcuffs lay on the ground.

CHAPTER FORTY-TWO

Riding the panicked crowd, Lucas wrenched Martina from the ground and pulled her into the throng, gripping her tight as he found his feet and kept pace with the stampede.

"Don't even think about losing me, Martina," said Lucas.

He held Sam over his shoulder, forcing the slower runners out of their way and dragging Martina along as they tripped over the fallen and bumped their way to freedom.

At the foot of the bridge, the police opened the barriers they'd installed to control the flow of people. Police horses moved to one side and, as far as Lucas could see, a sea of heads parted, making way for the thousands of people that sought escape from the bridge.

A right turn onto Lambeth Palace Road showed itself through a gap in the crowd and with a sharp pull on Martina's arm, Lucas followed hundreds of others to escape the rush into the comparatively empty piece of road.

Whistles blew and fluorescent jacketed police officers attempted to guide the roaring crowd with glowing batons. But the mass soon overcame them, forcing them to one side in time for Lucas to rush past.

The helicopter swooped low, shining its light and searching for Lucas, who diverted into a backstreet. He slowed to a walk, glancing over his shoulder to make sure they hadn't been followed.

"Where are you taking us?" asked Martina, breathless and frightened. "I can't run any further."

"We're going to where all this began," said Lucas. He stopped, pulled her wrist so she crashed into him, and then, with his hand still clutching the mobile phone, he ran his finger along her cheek. "Soon all this will be over."

He glanced over her shoulder at the buildings behind her, remembering a fourteen-floor office block with floor-to-ceiling glazing and an automatic revolving door at ground level that welcomed visitors and workers into a marble clad reception.

In its place was the shell of a building wrapped in scaffolding and green protective netting. In place of the automatic revolving doors was a wooden sign holding the name of a construction company and artistic renders of what the new refurbishment might look like.

"Follow me," said Lucas, pulling on Martina's wrist, offering her little choice in the matter. "And bring the bags."

He pushed a loose panel in the hoarding, holding it open for Martina and Sam to step through. Martina held both bags at arm's length as if they might go off at any second. Lucas followed and entered the construction site with Martina and Sam in tow.

The reception layout was exactly how he remembered it, minus the marble cladding, the long reception desk and the echo of expensive shoes. In their place were bare concrete walls, piles of acoustic insulation, the distant sounds of London and an eerie silence.

"I want to see Herman," said Martina. "I want to see him one last time."

"Well, you can't," said Lucas, as he searched for the stairwell. "Herman is weak. He's not to be trusted. I gave him the chance to finish it all and die a man. But he couldn't, could he?"

Darkness shrouded the concrete stairs. Broken bricks and concrete dust littered them, threatening to break a careless ankle. But with Martina in front and Sam between them, Lucas forced them up, floor after floor, until they reached the top. A hallway offered a choice of left or right. Old carpet still adorned the floor and the gypsum walls still stood, but all possessions and assets had been removed, ready for demolition.

Lucas turned left into the hallway. On his right was the shell of a single corner office where he remembered a large director's desk had stood in front of fine book shelves that were filled with leather-bound books and framed certificates.

To his left was an empty elevator shaft, dark and foreboding like the entrance to hell and from which a cold flow of air rushed, bringing with it the smell of damp and concrete. The void had been blocked with lengths of timber fixed across the opening and a yellow sign warning people of the danger.

Ahead of Lucas, only one office remained. Faint light spilled through the open doorway onto the carpeted floor as if it were welcoming Lucas home.

"In here," he called to Martina, pushing Sam ahead of him.

The room was smaller than he remembered. The smell of the demolition from the floors below and the perpetual city pollution that flowed through the empty window frame had tainted the fragrant sandalwood scent that accompanied Lucas' memories.

But it was the room. Of that he was sure. The two desks may have been removed and the vanity photos of celebrity meetings may have been relocated to a newer, shinier office, but it was the same room.

"Sit in the corner," said Lucas, when Martina stepped through. She clutched the doorway as if considering running. But with one hand on Sam's shoulder, Lucas eyed her, weakening the threat until she broke and stood in the corner furthest from the door.

"I said sit," said Lucas, as he gazed through the empty window frame.

She dropped into a defensive crouch with her arms around her knees. The bright moon and city lights lit her shiny, scared eyes from the corner of the room.

Lucas shoved Sam towards her.

"Is this it?" said Martina. "Is this where it all ends? In a crummy old office that's about to be torn down?"

"It's significant," said Lucas with a smile, remembering being led from the room in handcuffs.

"It's a construction site," said Martina. "It's hardly the glamorous ending I heard you boasting to Herman about."

"You don't deserve a glamorous ending," said Lucas. "After what you did to my brother, you cheating whore, what do you expect? A brass band? A last request? You'll get nothing but the ending you deserve and you'll be grateful I'm saving you from a lifetime of guilt and regret."

The comment roused Martina from where she slumped in the corner. She rose and stepped forward to put herself between Sam and Lucas.

"I did nothing wrong," said Martina. "We did nothing wrong. Your brother-"

"My brother what?" snapped Lucas, then paused to watch her squirm. "My brother is weak. But not for long. When I'm done everyone will see how strong he is. Nobody will remember him as the weak man that let some old man fiddle around with him and mess with his head. Nobody will remember him as the man whose wife slept around with whomever she wished. But to change people's minds, to alter their perception, takes work. It takes courage. And that's a courage Herman doesn't have."

Lucas made to leave the room, but Martina reached for his arm, digging her heels into the floor. He turned back to face her, outraged.

"He's not weak," said Martina. Then she let her voice trail away and her arms fell to her sides. "Not the man I loved. He was strong."

"Stop it," said Lucas. His face twitched and his eyelids blinked.

"Why should I? He's in there, isn't he?" said Martina. "You're keeping him from us, from his family."

"No," said Lucas, covering his ears. "Don't you talk to him."

"Herman, it's me," said Martina, offering him her softest voice. "Come to me, Herman. You're better than this."

"Stop," said Lucas. But his voice had already begun to weaken. His eyes widened and glistened with tears.

"That's it, Herman. That's it, my Herman. There you are. Oh, Herman. I love you. Come back to me."

"Don't say those-" Lucas began, but his voice weakened mid-sentence and his posture slumped. "Martina," he said, as if seeing her for the first time. He pocketed the phone and pushed a loose strand of hair behind her ear. "Do you mean what you say?"

"Of course I do," said Martina, her soft voice accompanied by a small fog as her breath met the cold and frigid air. "It's always been you. I missed you so much, Herman."

He turned as if he was unsure of his feet then stood before her, prepared for Martina to either attack or fling her arms around him.

"It's over," she whispered, stepping closer and laying her hand on his chest. "We're safe, and it's all thanks to you, Herman. You saved us."

She pulled away, holding him at arm's length to take in his face.

"What?" said Herman. "I didn't-"

"I just want to look at you," said Martina. "You did everything right, Herman. You were so strong."

"I was?" he said, searching through the cloud of memory but finding nothing. He looked around him. "Where are we?"

"We're safe," said Martina. "That's all that matters. Get us out of these bags."

"The bags?" said Herman, and a flicker of light shone across a dark area of his mind, a place he was forbidden to venture. "The bags? But I-"

"Herman, there's no time. We need to get out of here, but I can't run with this bag," said Martina, gripping him by the arms. "It's too heavy."

"No," said Herman. "I mustn't. I-"

"You're strong, Herman," said Martina, waving her hand at Sam.

"Look at what you did. You saved us. You saved your son. You're his hero."

Sam, who had climbed to his feet and was clinging to Martina's leg, looked up at Herman, his eyes wide with fear but pale just like his father's.

"My son?" said Herman.

"Yes, Herman. Help us get these off before it's too late."

"But Lucas-"

"Lucas is gone, Herman," said Martina. "You mustn't mention his name or he'll return."

The fog in Herman's mind thickened. The answers were there at the tip of his tongue. So much familiarity but so little clarity.

"The keys are in your pocket. You're in charge now, Herman. We have to stay strong."

He searched his pockets and found a small keyring with two keys. Holding them up to the moonlight that shone through the empty window, another memory flashed across his mind then vanished as quickly as it had arrived.

The crunch of broken glass on the carpet in the hallway stopped them both.

"Hurry," said Martina in a whisper. "Unlock the padlocks."

"Who's out there?" said Herman.

"It doesn't matter," said Martina. "Just unlock us, Herman. Save us. You're in charge. Remember?"

He snapped back to her then fumbled with the locks as the slow footsteps of a man grew louder in the quiet corridor outside.

"Quickly, Herman," said Martina, offering him the padlock with a frantic glance at the door. "Please."

But the key wouldn't fit the lock. The darkness and his shaking hands prevented him from finding the hole with the key.

"Hurry, Herman. Please," said Martina.

The footsteps stopped.

Herman's eyes narrowed.

"No," said Martina. "No, Herman. Come back."

Lucas straightened, clicking his back as if it ached from slouching. He found Martina staring up at him, aghast.

"Miss me?" he said.

Then he shoved her and the boy back into the corner as the body of a man fell through the open doorway fighting for breath.

CHAPTER FORTY-THREE

The old, worn carpet itched at Reilly's fingertips yet gave the sensation of electricity when his fists curled and unfurled. A string of blood hung from his lips and clogged his throat, barring the airway for clean air to reach his diminished lungs.

He dry-retched and spat the iron taste from his mouth before the first kick slammed into his chest.

"Don't you die yet, Reilly," said Lucas, and rolled Reilly onto his back with a hard shove of his foot. "Don't you spoil my game now, will you?"

The blood collected at the back of Reilly's throat, causing a coughing fit. Bloody, red mist flew from Reilly's mouth but his swollen airways restricted his breathing even more. In a panic, he rolled away from Hoffman onto his side, spat a wad of blood onto the carpet and focused on calming his breathing. Each deep breath allowed more air through than the last, slowing his racing heart.

He sensed rather than saw the layout of the room. A cold snap of wind on his back from the window at the opposite end of the room. The whispered murmurings of the boy. The whimpers of the woman huddled in the corner.

"So this is your big rescue, is it, DCI Reilly?" said Lucas. "I'll be honest with you. I'm less than impressed and I imagine Martina and Sam here are wondering why you bothered at all. Should have stayed at home with your hot chocolate, old man. Counter-terrorism is a young man's game, I'm sure."

"While there's life in these old bones, Hoffman, I'll be stopping people like you. It was what I was born to do."

"You conjure such a romantic image," replied Hoffman. Then he paused and Reilly could almost hear the smile on his pale face. "Do you recognise this place?"

With a final cough to clear his throat, Reilly rolled to a seated position, leaning against the wall to see Hoffman. His silhouette was dark against the bright night sky but his shape was unmistakable, lean and lithe, and almost feminine in the way he stood.

"Of course I remember it," said Reilly. "I have fond memories of walking you through those doors, and even fonder memories of slamming the door to the meat wagon that carried you away. What was it? Five years? We should have fought for a longer sentence."

"Parole is a wonderful thing," said Hoffman. "It's amazing what a little good behaviour will do, coupled with a thirst for knowledge. In fact, I should actually thank you for catching me when you did. If my original plan had succeeded, I would have ripped this floor off the building and taken Jasper Charles with it. But then I would never have learned the things I did, locked up in my little cell with my cell mate, whiling away the hours, listening to him teach me all the things he knows about..."

"About what?" said Reilly.

"Chlorine bombs. Their toxicity. Mobile phone technology. Everything I needed to know, Reilly. And all because you walked me through that door," said Hoffman. He gave a little laugh. "I'd probably still have half of my list."

"I would have caught you," said Reilly. "We would have, the force. One failed assassination plot may have opened doors for a smart lawyer to get you off, but not this time, Hoffman. This time it's for real. You'll never see the light of day again."

"That's interesting," said Hoffman, and he pushed off the window sill, disappearing into the dark corner where the woman sat with her son.

"What is?" said Reilly. "You're not interesting, Hoffman. You're sick."

"Exactly," said Hoffman. "I'm sick. We're sick. Both of us. Herman and me."

"Your brother is dead, Lucas."

"No," said Hoffman, stepping closer, quickening his pace to close the gap. "He's alive. He lives on. In me. I'm resurrecting his memory. I'm cleansing the world of the bad things he did."

"You're killing the reasons he did what he did," asked Reilly. "Isn't that admitting he was sick too?"

"He was weak. He was easily manipulated," said Hoffman. "There's a difference."

"Talk to me about Jasper Charles," said Reilly. "Tell me where he fits into all of this."

"You'd like that, wouldn't you?" said Hoffman, turning his back on Reilly. With his arms behind his back, he paced the room, turning on one heel to begin the return journey. "He's the one that started it all," said Hoffman. "He had the twisted mind of a man even weaker than Herman. A man so devious and evil, he built a small empire to shine the light away from his sick and perverse taste in young boys. Look around you. Do you remember how this place looked, Reilly? Do you remember the glass cabinets with the awards and photographs of him with the stars?"

"I remember," said Reilly. "He was a successful man."

"He was a successful man," said Hoffman, with a tone that conveyed his hidden smile. "Not anymore though, eh?"

"What about Jubilee Gardens?" said Reilly. "The first bomb?"

"Patrick Gervais," said Hoffman. "It was him that sent Herman under really. Jasper Charles may have started the whole thing, but by the time we went to school and Fatty Patty got hold of him, poor Herman didn't stand a chance."

"He bullied Herman?"

"He humiliated him. He distributed photos of Herman and..." He paused, as if unable to say the name again.

"Jasper Charles?"

Hoffman nodded.

"It scarred him for life," said Hoffman. "Can you imagine going to school every day with two hundred kids laughing at you? Opening wounds that you try to bury every night?"

"But you're his brother. Why didn't you help him?"

"I can't be everywhere," said Hoffman. "I spent my entire life looking out for that boy. Can you imagine spending every day worrying if today's the day that your twin brother, the other half of your own being, will kill himself?"

His voice softened and, for the first time, a trace of humanity showed itself like a weak sun behind black thunderheads.

"I've spent half my life keeping him alive," said Hoffman. "And the other half spent correcting his mistakes, erasing his past."

"Do you think it's time?" asked Reilly.

"Time for what?"

Reilly allowed a pause, time for Hoffman to tune into what he was about to say. He waited for Hoffman to stop pacing and turn to look his way.

"Do you think it's time to let him go?"

But Hoffman remained silent as if he was digesting the statement. Fighting the statement. Searching for a reasoned argument.

"You've helped him all you can, Lucas," said Reilly, as he pushed himself to his feet, one hand on his chest, the other steadying himself on the wall. "He must be looking down at you right now, smiling with the love that only a brother can have."

"No," said Hoffman, his voice almost a whisper. "No. Herman lives on. He's right here. He's with me. You can't take him away anymore. Nobody can."

"He's gone, Lucas. You have to let him go," said Reilly. "You've done it. You cleaned his memory. Let him fly. Let his name be remembered with smiles. Don't hold him back. Not now."

"I can't let him go," said Hoffman, snatching away to pace the room. The soft tones Reilly had drawn from him were replaced with bitter, snappy snarls.

"You've done it," said Reilly, raising his voice. He waited for Hoffman to turn away from him, gave the girl and the boy a quick glance and found them huddled together, eyes wide with fear and wonder, then pulled his handgun from beneath his jacket. "You set him free, Lucas. You set him free but you paid the ultimate price."

Reilly armed the weapon. The sound of the metallic slide was clear in the relative silence.

Hoffman stopped beside the door.

His head lifted.

"The ultimate price?" said Hoffman. He turned to face Reilly, testing his resolve.

"Stay where you are," said Reilly, his finger poised over the trigger and, for the first time in months, his hand was as steady as a rock.

"I suppose you'd like to be the one who walks me out of here?" said Hoffman. "I suppose you'd find some kind of cyclical satisfaction. I can see the newspapers now. The old photo beside the new."

"Take your hands out of your pockets and raise them over your head, Hoffman."

But Hoffman didn't comply. He didn't even acknowledge Reilly's demand.

"You remember what I told you on the bridge, Reilly? The others on the list were all for my dear brother, Herman."

He took a step forward.

"But you were for me."

"Hands, Hoffman," said Reilly. "It doesn't have to end this way."

"No," replied Hoffman, pulling his hands from his pocket. "No, it doesn't."

"Drop the phone," said Reilly, steadying his aim.

But the phone's green screen lit up.

"You're right," said Hoffman. "It doesn't have to end this way."

He hit the green call button.

In the corner of Reilly's eye, a second green screen lit up, somewhere in the corner of the room.

In the split second that Reilly connected the pieces and made a decision, the same split second that Hoffman winked at him and made towards the door, he felt death's presence looming above him like a cloud with long, spiteful fingers teasing at his dying body.

He bound across the room as the phone connected to the woman's backpack gave off its first ring.

An emotionless trill, three seconds long.

"One," said Reilly, as his hands found the padlock. But he couldn't force it open.

The screen flashed green again, accompanied by the same trill sound.

The girl looked up at him, frightened, frozen with terror.

With everything he had, Reilly pulled at the straps. But they wouldn't budge. He jammed his foot against the furthest strap, forcing the bag and the woman against the wall, and pulled on the second strap. There was a tear of fabric.

He pulled harder, his chest closing with the exertion. His airways tightened. He growled, giving every last ounce of oxygen he had inside his body to the muscles that tore at the straps.

And they ripped, sending him staggering backwards.

The green screen flashed on for the third time, lighting the side of the woman's terrified face in emerald hues.

"Get it off," he yelled, and launched himself at the girl. He pulled at the backpack, bending her arms back as the trill sound began its final alarm.

"It's stuck," she said.

Shoving her against the wall, Reilly tore the bag from her body.

But as he stepped away, clutching the bag against his own body, for the tiniest fraction of a moment, he found the boy's wide eyes, inquisitive, wide, and paler than any eyes Reilly had ever seen before.

Time seemed to stop.

The shrill tone stopped.

Somewhere on a digital switchboard far away, a pre-recorded voice message began to play.

Four uncertain eyes stared at the bag then up at Reilly, tears shining in the bright moonlight as the evil grip of his disease stabbed with its steely claws into his chest, closing his airways for good.

And with a silent acknowledgment to the woman, an unspoken passing of the gift of life, Reilly held the bag and launched himself through the empty window, and welcomed the solace and peace that awaited him on the hard concrete below.

CHAPTER FORTY-FOUR

Cold hands found Lucas' neck, hands with a strength fuelled by malice and unconstrained by doubt, fear or trepidation.

He dropped the phone on the old carpeted floor and grasped the cold hands. But instead of fighting, instead of grappling with the man's strength, Lucas held the hands in his own, caressing the hard skin until their fingers interlocked.

"Harvey Stone," said Lucas, through his constricted throat. "I knew you'd come for us."

As predicted, Stone pulled away, stepping back from Lucas but covering the exit.

"What are you going to do, Stone? How are you going to kill us?" said Lucas, taking a single step towards the man who had taken Herman's life, the man that who had haunted Lucas' dreams for five long years.

But Stone didn't reply.

"You could take us to Wimbledon Common? I know this place. You could bury me alive," said Lucas, taking another step forward. "Just like you buried Herman."

Stone took a single step back, keeping his distance, but his ever watchful eyes followed Lucas, reading him, waiting for a move.

"Don't you see?" said Lucas. "Whatever you decide and however you choose to do it, we win."

The words had no reaction on Stone's face. Although it was swathed in shadows and only a faint outline of his hard face could be seen, there was no variation in his expression.

"If you decide to bury us alive, they'll find us, and we'll win. If you decide to crush our skull with those strong hands of yours, we win. They know about you now, Harvey Stone. The whole world saw you on TV. So you can walk us out of here and hand us over to the police. Or you can finish it right here. Squeeze the life from our body. Either way, we win and you lose."

Stone didn't reply.

Lucas stepped forward, forcing Stone back another step.

"You're afraid," said Lucas. "The great Harvey Stone is afraid of losing."

He stepped forward once more. But Stone remained where he was. From his hand, a flash of steel caught Lucas' eye.

Lucas smiled.

"What are you going to do, Stone?" said Lucas, taking another step forward, taunting the man with opportunity. He stopped just two arms' length away. "Are you going to cut my throat? Are you going to cut me open?"

"How did you know where I buried him?" said Stone, his voice dry and cold like the blood that ran through his veins.

"Instinct," said Lucas. "We're twins."

"No," said Stone. "Tell me how you found his body. Tell me how you found Herman."

The mention of his brother's name woke something inside Lucas, a sadness that hung heavy on his heart, tightening his chest. Casting his mind back more than five years was easy. The images he recalled had haunted him day after day, night after night.

"Do you remember the rain, Harvey?" said Lucas, lowering his voice. "That night. Do you remember how it fell in sheets?"

Stone didn't reply.

"I do," said Lucas. "It's all I remember. The reflections on the wet road. Bright car lights and deep shadows, Harvey. Shadows deep enough to hide a grown man."

"You followed me?" asked Harvey.

"Just as you clung to the shadows, stalking my brother as a lion might stalk its prey, I followed you. I could have taken you then. I could have stopped you before you even touched him."

"But you didn't."

"No," said Lucas. "You fascinated me. The way you moved. The silence you never broke."

With his arms hanging at his sides, Lucas offered himself with no suggestion of attack or means of defence. Instead, he rode the ego of the man he'd dreamed about so often, his life on the blade of Stone's knife.

"At first, it was curiosity. I watched Herman leave through the window of our flat. I knew where he was going, of course. I knew what he was going to do."

"And you didn't stop him?" said Harvey.

"You didn't know him. Not like I did. He didn't mean any harm," said Lucas. "He didn't know any different."

Harvey didn't reply.

"That was when I saw you. You stepped from the trees in the car park. You followed him. Always behind. Always out of sight."

Somewhere, behind the eyes of the man, the night was being played out. Lucas wondered if a killer like Stone could recall the details at will, or if he managed to file the night away, compartmentalising the atrocities.

"Do you remember, Harvey?" said Lucas. "Tell me you do."

"I remember."

"Do you remember the Common? How you stepped through the trees, flanking poor Herman?"

"I do," said Harvey.

"And you remember forcing him to dig his own grave?" said Lucas, a taste of bitterness evident in his words.

"I do," said Harvey.

Neither man spoke for a few seconds. The scene played out between them. Memories. Flashbacks.

And for Lucas, tears.

"Can you imagine how it felt to watch you do such a thing?"

Harvey didn't reply.

"Can you imagine how it felt to watch my poor, dear brother's broken body being dropped into a hole? He was alive. Damn you," said Lucas. "He was still alive. There was a chance you could have stopped yourself. There was a chance he'd be alive now, instead of forcing me to carry him, sharing my body with his tainted soul."

"He needed to die," said Harvey.

"He needed a chance," said Lucas. "He needed guidance. You could have stopped."

Harvey didn't reply.

"All night, I sat on his grave," said Lucas, after a pause. "I heard his final cries for help. I felt his final breaths in the hose you forced into his mouth. And I felt the last beat of his heart in my own. I felt him join me, Harvey. I felt him enter me. I can see what he saw. I can feel what you did to him. The earth piling on top of him. The fright. The fear. The terror. Knowing that when that earth covered his face he'd never ever again walk this earth in his own mortal body."

"But you didn't stop me," said Harvey.

The words caught Lucas off guard. He stepped back.

"You didn't try to stop me," said Harvey. "You watched him dig the hole. You watched me break his bones. You heard him screaming. Tell me you heard him screaming, Lucas. Because I can remember it now. Right now. The noise is playing in my head. The tears. The begging. It's all here," said Harvey, tapping his temple with his index finger.

Lucas shook his head, shaking the thoughts from his mind.

But Harvey stepped forward once more, forcing Lucas back further. "You watched your own brother die and you did nothing. You sat on his grave when I'd gone and you did nothing. Tell me you tried, Lucas. Tell me you tried to pull him out of the hole."

"Stop," said Lucas, his voice high. He brought his hands up to his ears to block out the sound.

"None of this is for him, is it?" said Harvey, moving ever closer, rubbing the handle of his blade with a practiced finger. "This is all for you. This is all for your guilt. You watched your brother die. Your twin brother. The only person in this world you were supposed to care for and now you can't live with yourself. Can you?"

Lucas dropped to his knees, burying his head in his hands.

"Stop," he screamed. "Stop it. You don't know. You didn't know him. Not like me. Nobody did. He just needed love. He just needed showing."

"You killed him," said Harvey. "You killed him just as much as I did."

A flood of blood rushed to Lucas' head. A tightness overcame his mind. His thoughts whirled around, teasing him with the fragments of memories of Herman he'd clung to for so long.

But all clarity had gone.

The memories were lost to a wash of guilt.

He sat up on his knees and stared up at Harvey.

"Do it," he said, offering Stone his open throat. "Let me go to him. Let me find him, wherever he is. He needs me."

Harvey stepped forward.

He took a handful of Lucas' hair in his hand and held his head still.

A fierce light shone in Stone's eyes, ice blue and devoid of emotion.

"Do it," said Lucas, as he felt tears fall from his eyes and run across his pale skin. "You win, Harvey Stone."

But Harvey didn't move a muscle.

He waited.

Then he rolled his neck from side to side as if the stretching gave him some kind of relief of tension, allowing him to savour the moment.

Then his faced dropped and his knife hand shot into the air in a flash of light.

"Stop right there," said a voice.

Harvey froze.

It was female. Authoritative.

"Drop the knife, Stone," said the woman from somewhere close to the staircase.

"Harvey, do as she says," said another voice.

The command was supported by the sound of a weapon being armed.

But Harvey didn't reply. He held onto Lucas' head, knife poised to strike while behind those cold eyes, the odds were being weighed.

"Do it," whispered Lucas. "Finish it."

"Harvey, don't listen to him," said the second woman, as if she knew the man, as if she could get to him. "It's a trap, Harvey. If you do that, he wins."

"He needs to die," said Harvey. "They both need to die."

"That's not your call, Stone," said the first woman. "Drop the knife before it's too late."

"Don't come any closer," said Stone.

"Harvey, listen to her," said the second woman. "Please. It's me. Listen to her."

Harvey tensed.

His hand pulled hard on Lucas' hair, pulling his head back further, opening the neck up ready to slice. His face tightened with the power he was summoning for the strike.

Lucas closed his eyes, welcoming the kill. He thought of Herman. He thought of his face. His eyes. His soft touch.

And Stone's hand relaxed, releasing Lucas' hair from his strong grasp.

Lucas opened his eyes.

"Do it," screamed Lucas. "Kill me, you coward."

But Harvey lowered his knife. He took a step back.

Clinging to the thought of death, the chance of escape and the hope of being with Herman one more time, Lucas scampered across the floor on his knees.

Stone backed away and the policewoman stepped into view.

"Kill me, you coward," cried Lucas. "You killed him. Now kill me."

Lucas dropped his hands to the floor, burying his face into the old carpet to wipe away his tears and scratch the frustration from his angered mind.

As Stone stepped away and the policewoman stepped closer, Lucas backed away from her.

"Get away," he screamed, and stood to defend himself.

But the woman aimed her weapon at his chest, her stance strong and her hands unwavering. "Lucas Hoffman," she began. "I am arresting you on suspicion of murder on multiple counts. You do not have to say anything, but anything you do say-"

Her speech was interrupted by a scream to Lucas' left. From the doorway of the second office, Martina launched herself at Lucas, scratching at his face, tearing his skin with her nails and driving him back further and further towards the elevator shaft.

Teeth found skin.

Fingers pulled at hair.

And sharp claw-like nails found the soft flesh behind Lucas' eyes.

Until the crack of wood snapping stopped the attack.

And, as if the doors of hell opened up and swallowed him whole, he fell.

The slice of moonlight that shone into the corridor faded to a dot.

And Herman's smiling face grew bright and clear in the darkness until Lucas' body hit the bottom of the elevator shaft and the slither of the desperate soul he'd clung to for five long years was released.

CHAPTER FORTY-FIVE

Spinning, blue lights lit the narrow side street. Bright yellow jackets walked to and fro, some urgently, others less so. Uniformed officers had cordoned off the area creating a concentration of bustle and noise.

But there was a sense of relief.

Two paramedics pushed a gurney towards one of the two waiting ambulances. A sheet had been used to cover the body, but from the looks of disdain from each of the uniformed officers they passed, Harvey knew it was Hoffman.

Loading the gurney was unceremonious. The paramedics closed the rear doors, asked the senior officer in charge of the scene to sign a release form, and then pulled out of the crime scene with a police escort front and back. The blue lights flashed but they drove in silence.

Staring from the rear seat of a police car, Martina watched the ambulance leave. She wore neither the bitter look of hatred nor a look of dismay. Her face was blank as if she was coming to terms with a stain on her life being washed away. No matter the consequences, the Hoffmans were gone.

"How are you feeling?" asked Cole.

Harvey nodded, but said nothing.

"You're free to go," she said, and flicked her eyes between Harvey and Melody, who was standing by his side. "We have your statements and we'll be calling you in for further questioning during the enquiry. But as far as I'm concerned, we have everything we need until then."

Harvey opened his mouth to speak, but a clatter of metal to his right caught his attention. From the side of the building, two more paramedics wearing hazmat suits pushed a gurney towards the last ambulance.

Like the first, the body had been covered with a sheet.

But unlike the first, each officer stopped, removed their hats, and offered Reilly their own silent thanks as he passed them for the last time.

The senior officer raised his hand to stop the paramedics then glanced up at Cole as if he was seeking permission to remove the sheet.

Cole let out an audible breath then inhaled, filling her chest. Her eyes moistened as Melody reached out and touched her arm.

"Say goodbye," said Melody, as if the two were friends, connected on some level far deeper than Harvey knew of. "You'll always regret not saying goodbye."

Cole dizzied and closed her eyes.

But as the senior police officer went to push away Reilly's body, Cole spoke. "Connor," she called, then hesitated, finding the strength inside to do what she knew was right. "Wait."

The policeman offered her a look of sympathy and held out his hand for her to hold onto, offering his own strength.

"We should leave them to it," said Melody, and turned to face Harvey.

He glanced back at the construction site, looking up at the windowless top floor, and then cast his gaze across the rooftops and high-rise buildings that reached into the night.

Harvey nodded.

A uniformed policeman held the red and white tape up for them and they made their way onto the main road.

Cars honked in celebration. Drunken men and women linked arms, their collective mass spanning the footpath. Lights shone in every direction as Melody and Harvey reached the riverside where the ordeal had begun.

They found a spot on the bridge and gazed down at the inky water below, flowing regardless of the night, just as it had done during countless other horrific nights in the city.

"Life goes on," said Melody, as if she was reading Harvey's mind.

Harvey didn't reply. He nodded and met her eyes.

"Do I have to say I told you so?" she asked.

Harvey raised an eyebrow in question.

"I told you to let the police deal with it."

Harvey didn't reply. He stared down at the water.

"But I am proud of you, Harvey," said Melody. "I'm proud that you-"

"That I didn't kill anyone?" said Harvey. "I must be getting old."

"No," said Melody. "Not old. You're in your prime. I wouldn't change a single thing."

Harvey laughed, a single breath that produced a small cloud in the cold air.

"Do you think it's over now?" she asked. "Do you think we can relax now? Put all this behind us and start our new life? A new year. A new beginning."

"I'll try," said Harvey. Then he turned to her and smiled. "I can't promise anything though."

The first chime of Big Ben announced midnight and the new year.

The crowds that lined the riverside erupted into a giant roar. Arms waved, people hugged and the night sky exploded into life as the fireworks display began with a riot of colour and explosions.

But that was somewhere far away, somewhere that right there

and then, as Harvey stood with Melody by his side, faded with insignificance.

He reached out for her, pulling her in close and pushed a strand of hair from her face.

"I told you I'd find you, didn't I?"

Melody laughed. "I think you'll find I found-"

But her words were cut short as Harvey leaned in and found her lips. He kissed her with everything he had, everything he wanted to say but couldn't. Everything she needed to know was right there in that kiss.

It was as the last of Big Ben's chimes rang out that he pulled away, hovering close to her and leaning his head on hers.

"It doesn't matter who found who," said Harvey.

"No," said Melody, letting her arms find their way into Harvey's warm jacket. "But it's important to us that things will settle down. We need you around. We need you to be safe."

"We?" said Harvey, pushing her away a little so he could read her expression.

She smiled. For the tiniest of moments, uncertainty flashed across her eyes. But then they eased, and shone with tears of joy as her smile broadened.

"You're going to be a father, Harvey."

Harvey didn't reply.

The End

Also by J.D. Weston

Award-winning author and creator of Harvey Stone and Frankie Black, J.D.Weston was born in London, England, and after more than a decade in the Middle East, now enjoys a tranquil life in Lincolnshire with his wife.

The Harvey Stone series is the prequel series set ten years before The Stone Cold Thriller series.

With more than twenty novels to J.D. Weston's name, the Harvey Stone series is the result of many years of storytelling, and is his finest work to date. You can find more about J.D. Weston at www.jdweston.com.

———————

Turn the page to see his other books.

THE HARVEY STONE SERIES

Free Novella

The game is death. The winners takes all...

See www.jdweston.com for details.

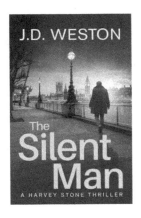

The Silent Man

To find the killer, he must lose his mind...

See www.jdweston.com for details.

The Spider's Web

To catch the killer, he must become the fly...

See www.jdweston.com for details.

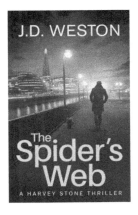

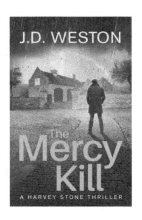

The Mercy Kill

To light the way, he must burn his past...

See www.jdweston.com for details.

The Savage Few

Coming 2021

Join the J.D. Weston Reader Group to stay up to date on new releases, receive discounts, and get three free eBooks.

See www.jdweston.com for details.

THE STONE COLD THRILLER SERIES

The Stone Cold Thriller Series

Stone Cold

Stone Fury

Stone Fall

Stone Rage

Stone Free

Stone Rush

Stone Game

Stone Raid

Stone Deep

Stone Fist

Stone Army

Stone Face

The Stone Cold Box Sets

Boxset One

Boxset Two

Boxset Three

Boxset Four

Visit www.jdweston.com for details.

THE FRANKIE BLACK FILES

Visit www.jdweston.com for details.

ACKNOWLEDGMENTS

Authors are often portrayed as having very lonely work lives. There breeds a stereotypical image of reclusive authors talking only to their cat or dog and their editor, and living off cereal and brandy.

I beg to differ.

There is absolutely no way on the planet that this book could have been created to the standard it is without the help and support of Erica Bawden, Paul Weston, Danny Maguire, and Heather Draper. All of whom offered vital feedback during various drafts and supported me while I locked myself away and spoke to my imaginary dog, ate cereal and drank brandy.

The book was painstakingly edited by Ceri Savage, who continues to sit with me on Skype every week as we flesh out the series, and also throws in some amazing ideas.

To those named above, I am truly grateful.

J.D.Weston.